Theodore Shurt

Lindsey

And Other Poems

Theodore Shurt

Lindsey
And Other Poems

ISBN/EAN: 9783337158385

Printed in Europe, USA, Canada, Australia, Japan

Cover: Foto ©Andreas Hilbeck / pixelio.de

More available books at **www.hansebooks.com**

LINDSEY

AND

OTHER POEMS

BY

THEODORE SHURT, M.A., CLERK.

---

*Poetry lifts the veil from the hidden beauty of the world,
and makes familiar objects to be as if they were not familiar.*

SHELLEY.

LEAMINGTON :

H. WIPPELL, VICTORIA TERRACE.

LONDON :

SIMPKIN, MARSHALL, & Co.

MDCCCLXXV.

CONTENTS.

PREFACE.

To publish verses is become a sort of evidence that a man wants sense.—SYDNEY SMITH.

IN the following pages, an attempt is made to treat the subject somewhat in a poetical way, and yet with regard to common sense. It may justly be doubted if the taste of the present age be not unhealthy, not to say depraved. The best poems in the English language were written many years ago by poets who, not only with genius, but with judgment, adorned their subjects with the finest figures of imagination, but, true to nature, kept clear of absurdities. In more recent times, one party have found satisfaction in rubbing up again the old, worn-out themes of heathen mythology— wasting much precious time and talent over the land where "beauteous error trod." Another party, treading on for- bidden ground, have been fond of dwelling upon subjects upon which, for the wisest reasons, nothing has been revealed to them or others. In speaking of heaven and spirits, they have rashly introduced a quantity of materialism and worldly furniture, and thus travelled into contradictions without any useful object. The tendency, of course, has been to en- courage a craving after forbidden knowledge, and a desire for what is fanciful and absurd. It is to be regretted that even some professing to be under strong religious impressions, have been led astray to treat upon such sacred subjects as if a special revelation had been made to them, and not known to the world at large. Even the great Milton, in his magnificent work, " Paradise Lost," when touching upon such subjects, becomes absurd. Sometimes his angels bleed, at other times they rise superior to the influences of space and matter. His failure might have been a warning to these ardent spirits to avoid such awkward themes. Celebrated heroes, giants, knights of the age of chivalry, imaginary kings, and other wonderful personages have had their day. Poems upon such subjects may be interesting, and to a certain extent instructive, but such themes have been almost worn threadbare. Even the " Tale of Troy divine " has been handled so often, and in such various ways, that with many it must be as stale as the death of Hector with a certain Roman Emperor. Two of our retired Prime Ministers, when divested of political power, have betaken themselves to Homer, and we will hope have found some satisfaction in adding to the number of the translators of the " Iliad." But this being a practical age, instead of going back into the beauties of ancient mythology, it seems desirable to bring before the public—if it can be done in an acceptable way—subjects that may conduce, directly or indirectly, either to the cultivating or the strengthening of the moral and religious faculties.

For a long time—up to about the time when Cowper's poems first appeared—poems upon religious subjects in the English language had proved, generally speaking, mere failures. So generally had this been the case, that the great lexicographer, Dr. Johnson, had come to the conclusion that all poems upon such subjects must necessarily be so, if the writer curbed his fancy and adhered to truth. Cowper, and since his time many others have shown that this dictum is not correct.

Certainly, a regard for truth and a pious dread of making too free with the Scriptures, must be a great check upon a lively imagination when a man is writing upon a religious subject. In that case he undoubtedly does labour under difficulties which the wild and luxuriant mind of a real poet would dread. Still, if he be really one who has the glory of God at heart more than his own petty, short-lived fame, he will value this obstacle at a low price. Pastoral poems have often been loaded with references to heathen gods and goddesses, which scarcely seemed in harmony with the minds of the Christian authors, or the sacred themes they dwelt upon. Such allusions the author of the following poems carefully eschewed. He had some difficulty in choosing between rhyme and blank verse. By way of variety he composed the Introduction in rhyme. It has been said by the editor of a modern poem of great and acknowledged worth, that poets are unwilling to admit how much the rhyme leads to the idea expressed. There may be truth in this. But, however great may be the help in this irregular way from rhyme, it must be far more than counterbalanced by the fetters which it continually imposes. Blank verse leaves full liberty for freedom of thought and imagination. The English language, from various causes, seems to be particularly well constituted for compositions in this style. These considerations induced the author to compose three Cantos in each Part of Lindsey in this style, and thus clothe his ideas in a garb suited to their rustic character.

Truth is the substratum of the poem entitled Lindsey. The object of the poem is to show that with very limited means, happiness to a certain extent may be obtained in some quiet, obscure places. This is shown by the contented

and comparatively happy lives led by some in Lindsey.` Of
those who attained to manhood, a very great proportion
descended to the grave in a good old age. "The fear of the
Lord is the beginning of wisdom ;" and this undoubted truth
the people of Lindsey recognised and exemplified. Hence
that moderate degree of happiness which fell to their lot
while they travelled on their way to a blessed eternity.

The names are formed from some connexion with the real
names of the persons they represent, or from some conspicuous
personal distinction of a creditable character.

It may seem strange to a hasty observer that the names
should be derived from so many languages—English, French,
Icelandic, Latin, Greek, and Hebrew—but it must be borne
in mind how mixed is the race to which they belong, and our
names which we use in daily life are quite as varied.

Many of the individuals alluded to might, to the writer's
knowledge, with much humility and thankfulness, have
applied to themselves the words of the Psalmist as we
find them in Psalm lxxi., from verse 12 to the end of the
psalm.

Leamington, Feb. 24th, 1875.

PART I.

INTRODUCTION.

IS there no place, O Albion, in thy bounds
  Free from the din of bustle, and the sounds
  Of jarring discord, and the feverish strife
  That dogs the steps of modern English life?
  No place where proud men with their haughty ways, 5
  Break not the even tenour of our days;
  Where lawyers never bring their tangled schemes,
  And misers of their gold indulge no dreams?
  Is there no village in whose calm retreat,
  Our days may pass in meditation sweet, 10
  Where undisturb'd by fashion's garish glare,
  Peace can be found, mix'd with but little care;
  Where love of lucre and the noise of trade
  Our wearied ears no longer shall invade?
  Yes, there are spots where yet the railway train 15
  Has never shot across the groaning plain,
  Spots dear to lovers of the rural scene,
  And rich in beauty, modest, and serene;
  Spots where the pastor and his flock unite
  And join in acts of kindness with delight: 20
  The pastor seeks in his unselfish plan,
  But God's great glory and the good of man;

Nor lends his office, like a traitor sly,

His own and others' whims to gratify.

And such wast thou, sweet Lindsey, calm, retired,   25

Known but to few, but by those few admired !

No dank canal cut through thy peaceful shades,

Nor railway whistle terrified thy glades :

No charioteering lords in pomp of pride

Along thy rustic roads were wont to ride,   30

But happy in his toil the simple swain

Talk'd to his horses whilst he drove his wain,

Free from all troubles of the great and gay,

Though not far hence the modern Corinth lay.

   Can nought but wonders please? The public taste, 35

Is it become so morbid, so debased

That few but wild imaginary schemes,

Beings that never lived except in dreams,

Can gain attention, or the mind depraved

Turn from the vanities it long has craved ?   40

Must gods and goddesses, such as of yore

A leading part in strains Homeric bore,

Be still the theme and fill the poet's page,

Where Christian deeds might well our thoughts engage ?

Ideal knights and damsels swell the song,   45

Angels of light and demons round us throng ;

4

Or heaven itself is enter'd, hell reveal'd,
And human pride would show what God conceal'd.
Draw back, my soul, from such presumptuous plan :
Content thyself with what God tells to man :   50
Ignore the glories of the pagan state :
Cull what we know the Scriptures do relate :
Israel's sweet Psalmist found enough to praise,
And with the truths of God adorned his lays.

Eternal praise attend my Maker's name,   55
Immortal harps His mighty acts proclaim !
Goodness and greatness dimly we behold,
Which e'en eternity cannot unfold.
Pond'ring on Thee, my God, my soul shall burn
And for Thy boundless grace show some return.   60
Let me in gratitude review in song,
When as an infant from the breast I hung,
The watchful love that hovered round my head,
And kept secure from harm life's slender thread :
Then bore me guarded through advancing years,   65
Bright'ning my hopes, dispelling all my fears,
Revealing in the earliest dawn of youth
The only way to happiness and truth.
Through manhood's stormy times, through all the wiles
By which the foe of God and man beguiles,   70

5

Thine arm hath held me safe, secure, serene
'Midst all the trials of this earthly scene.
E'en to hoar age Thy providential care
Hath been my guide, my safety, and my prayer !
And what, my God, what in return to Thee   75
For all the mercy Thou hast shown to me
Have I giv'n up ?   Alas, my conscious soul
O'erpower'd with shame looks back upon the whole !
Thy love did spare me, when in sinful pride
Thy will forgetting I had turn'd aside,   80
Unworthy even of the lowest place
In Thy paternal care, yet still Thy grace
Thus long hath spared me, foolish, thoughtless, wild,
Of sin and folly the ungrateful child.
Yes, oft will I look back through years long past,   85
And bless that God whose love will ever last :
Who pours on me each day a new-born flood
Of mercy, and ne'er tires of doing good :
And loads not me alone with gifts divine,
But showers His grace on every friend of mine :   90
Nor circumscribes His love.   His bounteous hand
Spreads blessings freely over all the land.
E'en on far-distant shores, earth's utmost bound,
Rich proofs of mercy everywhere are found :

Though man and Satan may combine to mar   95
His great designs, and sin His bounty bar,
Triumphant over all, with might sublime,
I see His goodness rise throughout all time.
But one great wonder towers above all thought,—
A world redeem'd and man's salvation wrought: 100
Deeds of transcendent worth are but as dross,
Paled in the splendour of that glorious cross :
And by the Holy Spirit the whole plan
Reveal'd and made available to man !
Oh, how shall worms of earth Thy might proclaim   105
In worthy strains, and magnify Thy name ?
Seraphs in vain to hymn Thy praise aspire,
The mighty theme o'erwhelms the heavenly lyre.
To some fair spot like Lindsey let me run,
And muse on what my gracious God has done: 110
Sweet Lindsey, loved of all—the rustic's pride—
Perch'd on the summit and the green hill-side,
Looks down o'er many a mead and lovely vale
That bare their bosoms to the western gale.
Spread to the view, seen from the churchyard height, 115
A rich expanse of verdure greets the sight.
No sterile heaths, no barren rocks are seen,
But joy and plenty crown the smiling scene.

At easy distance to the east, behold
The hoary town, where Alfred's child of old,   120
Though weak in sex, yet mindful of the foes,
From whom the troubles of her people rose,—
Rear'd a grim fortress, strong in art and place,
To curb the spirits of that Danish race.
The halo of old times still hovers round   125
The ancient site, and makes it hallow'd ground.
Those chiefs that once bore sway, and ruled the land,
And moved in splendour, in their day so grand,
Lost in the ocean of eternity,
Have only here a place in memory.   130
Their very forms, their grandeur, and their might,
And all the toys in which they took delight,
But dimly shadow'd in some ancient tale,
Scarce o'er the ravages of time prevail.
Gone are the mighty men, the stately dames,   135
And left no record even of their names.
Their bones are mouldering in the dust below;
Where rest their souls, 'tis not in man to know.
The woodlands echo with a kindred song,
And spring and summer dance the meads along :   140
Nature pours forth her charms, and laughs as gay
As when the rulers of old time held sway.

Shorn is the forest : many an aged oak,
Long known, has yielded to the woodman's stroke.
The children of the land more numerous grow ;   145
Less space is left for game and empty show.
Still, even now, high-bounding o'er the green,
Scared by some swain, the timorous hare is seen.
Up starts the partridge, with his ill-timed cry,
Before the horses as the plough draws nigh ;   150
And whirring from the brake, with outstretch'd wings,
Roused by the hedger's axe, the pheasant springs.
Few and less fierce, the wild of nature rove,
Through the rich cornfields and the neighbouring grove,
Mark'd by the peasant-boy, who notes with care   155
Where each shy creature loves to form its lair.
Wolves prowl no longer round the village folds :
His rural wealth secure the farmer holds.
Humble and joyful with contented toil,
Each evening sees the weary labourer smile,   160
Turn to his little cot, nor heed the world
With discord torn, in endless troubles whirl'd.
His is the happy mind, the lowly soul,
To feel no wish impatient of control ;
His foremost thought his wife and child to see,   165
Who hail his coming with unfeigned glee.

9

Then, on the Sunday, what sweet joy is theirs,
To worship God, all free from toil and cares.
The father in his livery smock so white,
The cheerful wife in rustic neatness dight.   170
Haste up the gentle hillock, from whose brow
The little church o'erlooks the vale below.
With lightsome hearts, young children round them run,
Their smart, gay dresses reddening in the sun,
Gentle and pleased, like butterflies that sip   175
The sweets of flowers, from various points they trip.
Sweet was the Sabbath morn: the sky serene
Look'd down in beauty on the pleasing scene :
A holy calmness hover'd in the air ;
Far off the world but near the house of prayer.   180
Then humbly kneeling in that blest abode,
How deep they felt the presence of their God !
Hush'd was the busy tongue, the wandering eye
Check'd by a kinsman or some neighbour nigh.
All watched their pastor as his place he took,   185
And knelt in prayer before the holy book.
Thus Sundays once began, serene and mild,
In Lindsey, loved alike by man and child.

CANTO I.

CANTO I.

Difficile est proprie communia dicere.—HORACE.

In Lindsey Church, beset with rotten pews,

Cold, comfortless, in rustic honours dight,

Nortonio stood and eyed his little flock.

This calm survey he took ere yet he stepp'd,—

Robed in a vesture of unspotted white,   5

Fair symbol of what piety should be,—

Forth to his place of worship, little raised,

So he might lead their prayers, and counsel give.

There, prominent amidst the pious swains,

Sat Possumus*, with hoary head reclined,   10

Conspicuous with his rosy face and smile.

Promnens and two strong sons there, too, were seen :

Domestic duties kept his wife at home,

Save when they met within that hallow'd house,

And the sun hastening sought the western sky.   15

Shrewd Anakson, grave, tall, in frame robust,

Sat there, and thankful felt he did not want.

There, too, sat Eric, with his lovely wife

And Christian-minded sister, all intent

---

* As a clue to the names, see the Glossary at the end of the Poem.

Upon their duties both to God and man,   20
In piety and mien distinct from all.
He was a man, to fashion's vain parade
Once known, but now the pearl of precious price
Himself and wife, and sister, all had found.
There, too, was Calvus seen—old soldier he—   25
Bald, venerable, like an aged oak
Reft of his branches, and his hoary top
Bleach'd by the northern blast : and close at hand
His daughter, Calva, dutifully near :
There, too, was Miles, his son, tall, slim, and gaunt. 30
Amnes his pallid face and bulky form
Uprear'd, and near his faithful partner sat—
Good, hospitable, thinking on the poor,
And wishful to be kind to all around.
Homo or wife was there : they dwelt of old   35
In that famed spot well known to honest clowns
Who loved on Saturday their well-earn'd ale.
Nor let the modern Pharisee turn up
His scoffing lip, and think how sad was this,—
That sweating hinds, who all the week had toil'd, 40
Should with such beverage recruit their strength,
Ease their tired bodies, and e'en thus prepare
To give one day to God in joy and peace.

Aubrey (of parish clerks himself he deem'd
The prime), was duly in his place, and bore   45
On his good-humour'd face looks most serene,
Of satisfaction with himself and all.
And in the gallery just opposite,
Confronting him with full-blown dignity,
Sat Snap, with violin, prepared to strike   50
The chords sonorous, singing as he played,
Like David with his harp of solemn sound.
Schoolmistress Sartor, with a loving train
Of fair young creatures, sat around the rails
That stood before the table of the Lord.   55
Such were the leading souls that seldom fail'd
To pay their homage to the Lord Most High,
And listen to the solemn words and truths
Nortonio publish'd from his rustic desk.
And whilst he spake in language plain, succinct,   60
All classes, high and low, both rich and poor,
Felt that he spake the truth, responsive felt
Their frames were mortal, but their souls should live,
When their frail bodies mingled with the dust.
All were attentive; all with reverence bent   65
And prayed, and sang and worshipp'd as they felt.
No hypocrites were there; no canting churl

13

Pour'd forth his penitence in sighs and groans.
Dissenters there were none : in holy things
They thought and acted as their sires had done.　　70
A learned priest they deem'd their own, and knew
Full well that he was college-bred, and train'd
In arts scholastic far above their ken.
And yet they loved to search their Book and see
How what he said agreed with Holy Writ.　　75
Himself encouraged this : he urged them on,
Taught them to seek th' unerring Spirit's aid,
Through Christ their great Redeemer, and the love
Of God the Father for His dear Son's sake.
He led their simple minds to think and judge,　　80
Prove text by text, and ponder on the truth.
This was the secret charm that held secure
Both priest and people in the bonds of love,
And bade defiance to the hosts of hell.

Memory, be thou my muse; say something more　85
Of those who took the lead in this small place,
And whom their brethren look'd to as their guides.
Small scope for pride was here ; 'twas better found
To live in peace, and love, and harmony.
In pleasant raillery, one was yclepp'd　　90
The squire, and two fair dames were dubb'd the queens,

And hence the lane in which they dwelt was styled
Queen-street. Few, e'en among the female tribe,
Their queenly wrath encounter'd : silently,
By hospitable deeds and timely gifts,   95
In sickness or some accident, they gain'd
All they desired, the homage of the heart.
   Nortonio was a man unique in mind,
Peculiar, fond of novelty and change.
He loved true wisdom ; from his heart abhorr'd   100
All that look'd like disorder, and pretence
Regarded with ineffable disgust :
Quick and discriminating, too acute
To dive full deeply into dry details.
The speechifier and the demagogue   105
Alike to him were objects of contempt.
Full well he knew the masses of mankind
Were gull'd and cheated by designing knaves,
And what is nicknamed popular applause,
He deem'd but incense fit for foolish pride.   110
Far different from some brother priests, he sought
No place of fame, no exaltation high,
But turn'd his back, in utter scorn, on means
Practised by priests in this degenerate age,
To gain a step in dignity or wealth.   115

If for this course you ask the reasons why,
One is enough—responsibility !
And yet had he aspired, he might have scaled
The ladder of ambition, and have fill'd
A post far more conspicuous : for his friends   120
Were numerous and potential, from the prime
Of England's peers and comm'ners to the swain
That lowliest sat beside the farmer's hearth.
And he possess'd some talent, and the power
Of talking till the wrong appear'd the right.   125
His mind was drugg'd with human lore, his wits
Sharpen'd and roused to constant vigilance,
But this he valued at small price ; for he,
Driven by the current of events, had found,
E'en in his youth, what Solomon in age   130
Discover'd, all was vanity at last.
His soul craved something better, nothing less
Than what he found in serving God alone.
His lot had varied been ; oft in the clouds,
Oft in the depths his soul was toss'd about.   135
Not seldom 'gainst his will he found a place
Where luxury and grandeur reign'd superb.
And often with the lowliest child of grief
He shared his sorrows, and the balmy cup

Of sympathy held out to anguish'd hearts,   140
A work congenial to his soul far more
Than flowing bowls and feasts of heartless mirth.
Thankful was he that he had found a place
Where he could minister in peace and love,
Uninterrupted by a carping world.   145
But thankful more was he that God had given
Grace to discern where he could labour best,
Both for his Master's glory and his own.
And yet he only fill'd the second place
In that small charge : mere substitute was he.   150
The vicar of a neighbouring church retain'd
The supervision of this little place.
But he, whom we shall call Clardonis, hail'd
Nortonio as a brother, and with love,
Superior to all jealousy and pride,   155
Most gladly welcomed to a share of toil.
He held the heavier charge, and overlook'd,
Not only on a Sunday, but each day,
The worship of his people, loved by all.
Six days in seven Nortonio labour'd hard   160
To train his pupils for their future toils,
And send them forth, not only armed complete
With arts and science, and the learned lore

That Greece and Rome could furnish, but prepared
To serve their God in every walk of life.   165
    Good-natured Possumus, in rural pride,
Lived happy on the land his own strong arms
And steady toil had earn'd : land which had once
Been almost profitless, but now by care
And diligence unwearied had been brought   170
To thrice the value that it held before,
When first he raised a loan upon that farm
To buy the freehold.   There, with two brave swains
To help him in the culture of his land,
And an old housekeeper to tend his house,   175
He pass'd through life contented. Liberal, too,
As well became the Warden of the Church,
His house was open at all proper times,
To hospitable rites and welcome friends,
But most on Sundays : on those holy days,   180
Boil'd leg of mutton was his favourite joint.
Ho, then he loved his minister to come,
With godly conversation share his feast,
And set the parish right for all the week.
Nor were the poor forgotten : well he knew   185
Who merited his favours, and he gave
Proportion'd to their industry and worth.

Each of the two old labourers enjoy'd
Full many a dinner in that house, and quaff'd
Cups of cold buttermilk, or cyder clear :   190
More rarely ale or beer rejoiced his heart :
And three half-crowns paid for his weekly toil.

  As for old Calvus, he had time to think
Upon the follies of mankind, retired
And closeted within his calm abode.   195
Caught with the love of military pomp,
Like many a crowned fool, his life had been
Spent 'midst the noise of arms : and empty fame
Had well-nigh led him to the brink of ruin.
A regiment to resist his country's foes   200
Himself had raised, and so a great exploit
He thought he had perform'd : but, thus o'erlook'd,
That what he did was done to gratify
His own peculiar whim. If he design'd
Simply to serve his country, that he could   205
More fully have effected, had he curb'd
His own ambition, and the nation's cause
Maintain'd and strengthen'd in the usual way.
His substance wasted and his children press'd
By poverty's hard trials, much he thought   210
Upon the past : what might have been perform'd,

Had he view'd differently this changeful world:
Or had the ungrateful nation valued more
His gallant efforts to uphold its fame.

    Then there was Promnens, sturdy yeoman he,   215
Who blest with solid sense, contented heart,
And humble spirit, in the sight of God
Most prec'ous, till'd his acres, some his own
And some his brother's. Tom and Harry, too,
H's lus'y lads, though young and but mere bo,'s,   220
Shared in their father's energy and care.
He dwelt in that old house, in days of yore
Where lived a sapient coun-ellor, well skil'd,
In human laws, to wrangle and define
Most technically; but in common sense   225
Strangely deficient, as his conduct show'd,
When cruelly, to gratify his pride,
He urged his steed o'er miles of half-form'd roads,
From London's Tower to distant Avon's banks.
The sun was shining when he left the bounds   230
Of England's capital, and ere the n'ght
Had thrown her mantle o'er the Lindsey fields,
He reach'd his home and triumph'd in his c'e ad,
Boasting, vain man, of what his horse had done!
Ill-fated animal, thy lot was sad,   235

To fall into the hands of such a wretch :
The next day brought an end to all thy pain,
And rescued thee from tyranny by death.
Great contrast to this lawyer—proud, austere—
Was simple-minded Promnens.   He possess'd   240
But little human learning : yet his heart,
Chasten'd and sober'd by the grace of God,
And sacred lore he in his Bible found,
Enabled him to lead a quiet life,
Above the turmoil of a restless world.   245
Deeply attach'd was he to church and state :
And though he might not feel himself prepared
To combat difficulties or decide,
By subtle argument or cases apt,
The intricacies of schoolmen and divines :   250
Like his own bull that roam'd his pasture round,
And kept from all encroachment stranger beasts,
He stuck to his old princ'ples, abhorr'd
All modern fallac'es and Romish views.

      Barbats, his brother, near on Blacon top,   255
H'gh and con-picuous far to east and north,
In peace and love with all his neighbours lived.
      Not far from him dwelt Anakson, a man
Of mighty energy.   'Twas said of him,

No idle clown need go to him for work,   260
Active was he from morn e'en to late eve,
And ate the bread of carefulness, intent
Not merely to save money, but to give
To every one his due ; and as he paid,
So he required returns in honest toil.   265
Like some strong branching ash-tree, placed beside
The public road, throwing out his arms above,
And intersecting with his roots the ground
Which otherwise would useless be for growth
Of foliage, by incessant care he throve ;   270
And flourish'd, too, where less industrious men
In disappointment would have closed their schemes.
Sore plagued had he been by the lawyer tribe,
Who harried all his gains for many a year.
No wonder was it that his neighbours thought   275
He cut things close, when thus the toiling man
Found the results of all his daily care,
Perverted and applied to fatten those
Who feed upon the weakness of mankind.

    With these her peers, and a long train besides   280
Of loving sons and daughters, blithe and strong,
Nursed in the lap of ease and peace profound,
And crown'd with plenty, Lindsey flourish'd fair ;

Obscure, unnoticed, whilst the outer world
Was torn with revolution, mad designs,   285
Religious fury, jealousy, and rage.
There, in the heart of England, safe she lay,—
Safe from all foreign foes, safe from the taint
Of restless spirits and the scheming crowd.
Few of her denizens e'er saw the sea,   290
Or hoped to see it, though they heard with joy
Of British triumphs, and the conquering fleets
That rode victorious round their sea-girt land.
Few, too, indeed, to visit had presumed
That famous town upon the banks of Thames,   295
Of which they heard such wonders, and e'en saw
With their own eyes the terrible details
In some stray journal that had come to hand.
The great emporium of the Midland shires   .
Was not far distant. To that toiling hive,   300
Perchance for business or some other cause,
One from the village would his journey take ;
And bring word back how there his senses keen
Had injured been by noise and smells most foul :
How, too, the people raved on things of state,   305
On politics, on subjects far removed
From understanding, till the dire debate

23

Confounded reason, charity, and truth.
Strange tales, too, brought he of the railway world:
How huge, loud-snorting engines tore their way,   310
And traversed distances, as far in length
As from the village to the Midland Mart,
In half an hour, instead of half a day,—
Their usual pace. Much did th' astonish'd swains
. Admire, but seldom cared to see,   315
This wonder of the age, or try its power:
Four miles from home was all some dared to go.
They recollected, and with loving care
Caution'd each other, how that two had gone,—
One to the wars, and one his country's laws   320
To guard at home. The soldier once return'd,
And then departed, ne'er again to see
Parents or home. Full many a month and year
Watch'd his sad mother, ask'd and sought in vain
For some slight clue to find her absent boy.   325
Rumour at length the intelligence conveyed,
That battles had been fought, and 'midst the list
Of kill'd in action, something like the name
Was found in an old journal, as opined:
Maternal instinct soon confirmed the guess.   330
As for the other, he at times return'd,

24

But not improved, as all his fellows thought;
And discontented with a rural life,
Stayed but short intervals and went his way.
Such sad experience deep impression made   335
On startled villagers, and even led
Some youthful spirits, that had dared to talk
Of seeing the great world, to pause and think,
And rest more happy in their humble sphere.

END OF CANTO I.

CANTO II.

CANTO II.

Perpetual motion in the wheels of time,
Soon brought Nortonio to the early close
Of his first year among his Lindsey friends.
As springs the school-boy from his hated bounds,
Jocund, exulting in a youthful dream   5
Of mirthful weeks enjoyed without alloy,
In his dear home amidst his kindred group :
As leaps the terrier when, with heart elate,
He bounds before his master in the fields,
And snuffs the breezes of the coming spring :   10
As the young linnet, after many a vain
And hopeless struggle to escape the bars
Of the dire cage, meant for his future home
By would-be friends on selfish pleasure bent,
Finds at the last an exit, and aloft   15
Pours forth his soul in liberty and bliss :
So joyed Nortonio, when to Lindsey's bowers,
From the proud suburbs of the Garden Town,
He bent his way, all free from books and care.
In that luxurious place full of vain arts,   20

C

Mean imitations of the great and good,
Fanatic zeal, professions loud and fierce,
And fruitless efforts to combine in one
The cause of pleasure, Mammon and of God,
Nortonio lived, and kept with care aloof   25
From all their factions and distorted schemes.
Strange was the medley, that he saw around
His daily movements in that upstart town,
Chaos of folly, vice and luxury.
And yet some small admixture of the good   .   30
Could there be found : some salt of Christian truth
Saved from entire corruption the whole mass.
A land of loveliness stretch'd far and wide
On all sides round the town—There nature's God
Had pour'd His bounty with unsparing hand.   35
Umbrageous trees, green meads, salubrious streams,
And balmy gales, health-bearing, soft and pure,
Sweet solace brought to charm both man and brute,
Art too, by various means, these treasures placed
In easy distance from the world around ;   40
So that from towns of greatest eminence,
And many a lonely hall, came hither oft
Those who sought ease for body or for mind.
No joy in this frail world can perfect be.

Alas! the lovely scene soon caught the eye   45
Of quacks, of harpies, male and female fools.
Thither in swarms they flew, and locust-like
Marr'd the fresh beauties of the rising Spa.
Pleased was Nortonio to escape the din
Of such a motley crowd, and refuge find   50
In Lindsey's quiet shades, and converse hold
With her poor swains untutor'd but sincere.
He took them to his heart and gladly found
A quick response of feeling pure and kind:
The golden key of love unlock'd their souls.   55
What might have raised their scruples, now was shut
In silence.   Freely full assent they gave
To him who drew them with affection's cords.
Oft had he struggled in the dark back streets
Of some hugh town, or e'en in London dens,   60
To cope with vice and hardened sinners bring
To some slight knowledge of their future state:
Oft with the discontented infidel
Points he had argued; and to sceptics proud
Imagined difficulties had explain'd: 65
And after all his labours fortified
By all that wit and learning could devise,
Gain'd from the wrangling tribe, untired with strife,

Consent reluctant, acquiescence vain.

Rapt was Nortonio's heart, when thus he found   70

A people willing to receive the truth

Of God in all humility and love.

Charm'd with the loved idea he rejoiced

And revell'd in it with luxurious joy.

Farewell then to all visionary schemes,   75

To wild ambition, to the dazzling bribe

Of admiration, to the vain applause,

Of crowds of erring sinners like himself.

Henceforth his soul congenial scenes should know

And labour where his labour was esteem'd.   80

And if no guerdon of high fame, or meed

Of popular applause, his efforts crown'd,

He had what more he prized ; love as sincere

And sweet as issued from a mother's breast.

There too unnoticed he escaped the gibes   85

Of clerical dictators, and the sting

Of would-be critics. As for bishops, he

Who then bore sway, had weighty cares that call'd

For his at'ention in the larger towns

And parishes around, besides the toil   90

Of planning schemes how to increase his hoard,

And twist his olive-branches round the seats,

Aristocratic deem'd, in times like these
And in a selfish world, no easy task.
Disturb'd not then by qualms episcopal   95
And meddling rulers, proud of public note,
People and priest, contented with their lot,
Managed their matters in a rural charge.
A scintillation of that holy flame
That glow'd in Paul, now fired Nortonio's soul,   100
And raised his mind above the vain pursuit
Of self, to labour for another's good.
To give than to receive more blessed far
His Lord had said, and he the truth had found.
Nor deem'd he it a point of foremost thought   105
Only to guard their souls : their bodies too
And worldly matters claim'd his watchful care.
By conversation he this purpose gain'd.
Observant closely of what pass'd around
Both near at home, and in more distant fields,   110
He saw much time and labour misapplied ;
Or only so applied as to result
In crops inferior and the land half till'd.
But most with Possumus, as old, inured
To ancient usage, was the theme discussed.   115
" How comes it, worthy Warden," thus exclaim'd

Nortonio, "that while rents and rates thus press
So heavy on the produce of the soil
As you describe, yet corners large and wide
All guiltless of the plough in many a field   120
Unfertile lie, while clumps of nettles too
Grow strong and rank and useless clog the ground."
" The corners that you speak of," thus replied
Contented Possumus, " a purpose serve
To give fresh vigour to th' exhausted land.   125
Our sheep must there be folded and rejoice
To find a patch of ground with verdure clad.
As for the rent, thanks to the grasping soul
That drove my father tenant from his farm
None have I now to pay.—His tyranny   130
Led me all landlords to distrust, and seek
By toil and care and borrow'd means to buy
Land that I could improve and call my own.
As for the horrid nettles, they will grow
As well as grass: when mown, they spring again ;   135
And if cut up by ploughshare or by spud,
The turf now firm by age, and rich in grass,
Would be disturb'd and spoilt for years to come."
" Then let your hind with bludgeon thick and strong,"
The parson said, " bruise well each nettle stalk   140

And every leaf belabour on the ground.
If thus the tops you kill, the root will die
And then the grass from all obstruction free
Green with fresh verdure will delight your flock.
I well remember when in eastern shires   145
Where Ouse slow-eddying rolls his turbid tide
It was my lot to live.   The farmers there
Made shafts some eight or ten feet deep and hurl'd
The silt and moist deposit that had lain
For ages at the bottom to the top ;   150
And thus an artificial surface form'd
So good, that if the process were renew'd,
But thrice in fifteen years, luxuriant crops
Of wheat and oats alternate well repaid
The farmer for his toils, and tripled oft   155
The value of the land on which he wrought.
Thus men well-known for industry and skill
Could often borrow all the land would cost
At first, and after fifteen years thus spent
In getting from beneath, what once was fen,   160
That mixture of marine and shelly clay,
Which mingled with the surface made the soil
So fertile, each acquired a goodly farm,
Well worthy of his judgment and his skill.

But now in matters of my flock give aid.   165

Grieved am I, Warden, to behold so few

On sacramental Sundays round the Board

Of our dear Lord, commemorate that death

And blood most precious shed for sinners' souls.

And yet at Clarebrook* close at hand, where once   170

It was my privilege to serve as here,

The pastor of a few contented souls,

Communicants there were, more numerous far

Than bore a fair proportion to th' adults,

That dwelt in that small village. Well, I deem,   175

They valued what their Lord had done for them:

And neighbours in the holy banquet join'd.

Here on that solemn day, when most of all

They should His temple fill, they stop away

Or turn their backs upon His feast ingrate."   180

Then said the farmer: "With sincere regret

Myself have noticed that so few attend

That holy ordinance; but still I claim

Some credit for the people of this place,

Who fear their God, and live as if His eye   185

Were always on them, which indeed is true.

My men have labour'd now full many a year

---

* See Glossary at the end of the Poem.

Early and late. My interest has been theirs :
And Aubrey, now your clerk, a prize has gain'd
For long and steady service on this farm—   190
But as you speak of Clarebrook, tell me now
How fared it with old Woven,* that grave man,
The Squire and Pastor of that parish once,
When you his substitute supplied his place.
He was, as you well know, beloved by all,   195
Who served or knew him ; hospitable, kind,
And generous to a fault. His largest farm
My brother occupied and found in him
All that he wish'd in landlord or in friend,
Far different from some landlords I have known."   200
    " The man you speak of was a godly man
Worthy of all esteem," replied the priest.
And well I ween the poor his loss lament
As squire and pastor both. That fair estate
That comprehended every stick and stone   205
In Clarebrook bounds, the Church, the land and all
His ancestors had held without a break
E'er since that king, whose bones in Worcester rest,
Ruled o'er the land. Deep and sincere the grief
That seized on all who tenanted the soil   210

* See Glossary,

When first they heard the news too sad, too true,
That to a stranger he had sold the place,
Although that stranger was a worthy man,
And one who had means, will, and talent too
To push improvements for the good of all.   215
With silent pleasure oft I call to mind   .
Last time I saw that venerable man,
And stayed beneath his hospitable roof,
And help'd to make arrangements then required
Both in Church matters and his changed estate.   220
His memory brought him back to other times.
He told how in his youth fair Tardaton,*
The Garden Town, now gay in pomp and pride,
With wide right-angled streets of fashion full
And crowded with the cavalcades of wealth,   225
For forty thousand pounds could all be bought ;
Advowson, freehold, every stick and stone :
And now a million could not compass all.
Then to his native Clarebrook he recurr'd
And told how pester'd with attorneys, bent   230
On selfish gains, the mortgages call'd in,
Urged he had been with added toil and loss
To raise fresh funds and cumber thus the land,

---

* See Glossary.

Till wearied with the strife he made short work
By selling all his land, although th' estate   235
For centuries his family had held.
Worn out the race was: children he had none;
His brother old and childless like himself.
The right name of his family had long
Been discontinued.   An old ancestor   ,   240
Sold cloth, and travell'd through the country roads
Impassable by vehicles, with teams
Of pack-horses, tied head and tail together.
Welcome to all the villagers was then
The foremost horse's head, when tired and slow,   245
Through dreary lanes wet with autumnal showers
To daylight he emerged and snuff'd with joy
The smell yet distant of the village inn.
Not only cloth was brought, but news as well.
Joy seized the villagers when first they saw   250
The foremost horse's head, and all exclaim'd—
" Here comes the Woven."   Hence his name disused
They hail'd him Woven, and as years roll'd on
Still Mister Woven was to all most dear,
Both for his cloth and for his news beloved.   255
From this distinguish'd scion of the race
Sprang a long line of progeny renown'd,

That filled in Clarebrook for some centuries
The post of squire or priest with little change,
Save that the pomp of shrievalty at times   260
Adorn'd some layman, or disturb'd awhile
That holy calm hereditary there.
Then to the times when his own grandsire built
The parish church the old man turn'd, and told
How when the structure had been raised, he gave   265
Land to provide for ministerial wants,
Land too which then produced an annual rent
Of seventeen pounds ten shillings : in that age
No despicable sum, though likely now
To call forth ridicule or raise a smile.   270
Then to his hounds the venerable sage
Referr'd, and told how his forefathers sought
Health and amusement in our rural sports,
Free from the taint and luxury of towns.
As for himself the cant of modern times   275
Moved not : with grateful heart he lived and bless'd
That God who gave him to enjoy so well
This life and look with chasten'd hope and faith
Through the rich merits of a Saviour's love
E'en to a better in that world to come.   280
Priest as he was, he loved his pack of hounds,

And in few words declared his health required
Such recreation, need not less to him
Than food of mind or body, such his wont.
Through his well-order'd house a spirit pure   285
Of piety and charity prevail'd.
Early each morn, ere to their daily task
His household turn'd, he as their priest besought
The Lord, and craved a blessing on their toil.
And nightly as the labour of the day   290
Closed in, assembled in the servants' hall,
His menials stood prepared to join him there
In earnest worship at the throne of grace.
Love made them his in heart, not name alone.
Consideration for their little wants   295
And all their ailments was his constant care.
His huntsman, when disabled by a wound,
Caused by collision in the hunting field,
Bless'd not his luck as some half-heathens do,
But thank'd his God, to whose kind providence   300
He felt himself indebted for the boon
Of having such a master. When the chase
He still could follow, though not yet restored
To perfect health, still with paternal love
His master watch'd him, and would not permit   305

The man to clean his hunter, lest th' attempt
Should mar his health or make the cure less sound.
I need not tell you how this worthy man
Held in the hearts of all his farmer friends
The foremost place. Full many a silver cup   310
He gave to call their competition forth
And crown their efforts to improve their farms;
Cups that are kept now with religious care,
And so to generations still proclaim
His generous heart and the receiver's praise.   315
Welcome was he with all his steeds and dogs
To urge the chase and scour the country round,
Studded with lovely woods, plantations thick,
That topp'd the gentle hills, and yet left bare
An open country for the sportsman's work.   320
E'en from the banks of Avon, Shakespeare's land,
To where dark Severn in his stately pride
Rolls by the towers of Wulftan,* our old friend
Could pass uncheck'd with all his hunting train.
No ancient patriarch in the days of old   325
Was dearer to his kinsmen or more loved
Than by the farmers was this aged priest.
And well it might be so : reciprocal

* See Glossary.

40

Was their esteem. They knew him as their friend
As well as priest and magistrate; and he   330
Watch'd for their good in this world and the next.
Pious and humble, though of ancient race,
Not only honour'd but beloved, he lived
A terror only to the poacher tribe.
Yet would he check an upstart in his pride   335
And seasonably keep him in his place.
If in his hot young blood some lordling rode
Careless and trampling on the crops now grown
Too much to bear such treatment without loss,
If after mild remonstrance, he resumed   340
This reckless course, the master gave the word
And forthwith huntsman hounds and horses all
Were hurrying homeward on the well-known road.
Well I remember when we rode along
Obedient to the bishop, who had call'd   345
This worthy man his conduct to explain
And give a reason, why he held a cure
Of souls at Clarebrook and yet made his home
Some twelve miles distant from that parish church,
He spoke with glee how with the love of all   350
And hearty welcome of his neighbours round,
He and his dogs could traverse that fair land.

Clarebrook was blest with many a rural charm,
But no sweet vicarage with a lovely lawn
And smiling garden was its pastor's lot.   355
And mindful what his family had done
Through ages for that place, the people too
Contented, thriving, but few very poor,
And those well cared for by the richer class,
It seem'd an act ungracious thus to chafe   360
Our aged friend, an act not wise indeed.
Since to the priest no house had been assign'd
There to reside the law did not require.
The prelate graciously received us both :
But soon a look uncomfortable spread   365
O'er all the bishop's face : he writhed and winced
Sore at the tauntings of the stern old priest.
No match was he for our quick-witted friend,
Who soon reversed the state of things, and sat
As arbiter of what was right and charged   370
Right reverend ears with truths unpalatable.
Signs unmistakable the bishop gave
To bring the skirmish to an end, but once
Our vicar roused, no quarter would he give
Nor cease till fully to his heart's content,   375
He had unbosomed all he held in store

It was a strange unseemly spectacle
For me, a young man, recently ordain'd
To this my holy office, to behold
Those men with sparring tongues and angry eyes,   380
Two gentlemen, and one a prelate too,
And one who always with a father's love
Guided my youth and inexperienced years.
That large square face, where kindness beam'd serene,
At other times, now pale with ire suppress'd   385
Confronted the cow'd bishop with fierce looks.
Alas, the duel was a bootless one.
The bishop, a smooth courtly gentleman,
Kind, with but little learning and no wit,
By whiggish interest and a brother's art   390
Placed as a ruler of the nation's Church,
To combat arguments such as our friend
Advanced, was ill prepared.   And he was known
To be well-skill'd in polemics and law.
Of all the treatises I ever read   395
On Confirmation his was far the best.
Complying with the vicar's wish express'd
I went as his companion to this scene,
And sat a silent hearer in dismay.
With joy unfeign'd the bishop saw at last   400

The old man rise up from his seat and turn
His huge broad back and slowly seek the door.
Glad too was I to see him safe beyond
The palace-gates, inhaling the fresh air.
Tall Malvern purpling in the distance shone   405
Lit by the evening sun, and mantled round
With rosy clouds that cheer'd us on our way.
But whilst we walk'd along the carriage road
Straight from the palace to the city streets,
The vicar glanced at former times, and told   410
How different bishops had become, since he
Himself was chaplain to a godly man,
Who wore a mitre in this very place.
" Once they were hospitable, glad to see
Their clergy, g'ad to comfort and sustain,   415
But," added he, " a dinner we shall have
Not in a bi-l op's palace but an inn."
So to the Ha'e and Harriers off we went,
And fared as sumptuously as heart could wish.
Then in his lumbering coach we took our way   420
And. God be pra'sed. return'd in safety home.
And i ow, good Warden, tired no doubt are you,
With this discourse : but well you know, if once
You set my mind in motion on this theme,

It is a labour to restrain my thoughts. 425
But time now tells me, homeward I must go,
And close my tale by bidding you farewell.

END OF CANTO II.

Hoar winter sullenly retired, and slow
Relax'd his grasp upon the frost-bound fields.
Spring peep'd forth shyly, and the woodland choir,
Their light hearts panting for connubial joys,
Chirp'd cheerily but check'd; nor yet secure   5
Caroll'd in all the ecstacy of song.
Snow hover'd in the air: in flakes at times
It tipp'd the summit of the neighbouring hills.
Sharp winds were scudding with the April showers
Oft tempered by a sudden glare of light   10
Shot from the opening sky. Thus cold and heat
Combined and softer'd the relaxing earth.
Winter and Spring by turns some trying weeks
Uncertain empire held, till now the time
Approach'd, so dear to every Lindsey child,   15
When relatives and friends from distant parts
Came trooping in to celebra'e the wake.
At length the sun pour'd from his eastern throne
A flood of golden light, and led the day
In all its beauty, full of genial warmth,   20

46

The meads bespangling with the pearls of dawn.
Joy touch'd the heart of Lindsey : joyous all
Her sons and daughters hail'd the vernal morn,
And blessed the Giver of all good, who bade
His clouds drop fatness o'er the laughing land.   25
Mirth spread contagious : flew from man to brute.
The stupid heifer that had brooded long
O'er heaps of cold dry fodder, till her limbs
Benumb'd and stiffen'd scarce would move at all,
Throws off her lethargy, and bounding forth   30
With tail erect extended o'er the back
Runs bellowing through the fields. The woods and hills
Reverberate, and answer with their glee.
Roused by the spirit of the time, the colt
Shakes his rough coat, and ragged mane, and springs 35
In youthful rapture o'er the sounding plain,
Scaring th' astonish'd lambkins, scattering wide
The bleating playmates, and their grave-faced dams.
Alas ! the bliss is fugitive : short-lived
Must all our pleasures be : 'tis so decreed   40
By God all-wise, for here is not our home.
Ten thousand secret causes all at work
Perpetually, by night, by day, conspire
To frustrate all the schemes that man would form

47

Of during happiness. He toils and strives,   45
Builds up an edifice of pride and wealth ;
And knowing that his stay must here be short
Looks for an heir to carry out the plan.
Then calls his lawyer to his aid, and schemes
How immortality can be acquired   50
For this his cherish'd dear design—Fond fool !
To think that wit of man can contravene
What God has order'd and declared shall be.
No such ambition shared the Lindsey folk,
Nor e'en their children. Happy for the time,   55
Contented with their lot and thankful too,
Proud of their village, deeming in their thoughts
No other parish equal to their own,
They earn'd that comfort and enjoyed it well
Denied to riches, luxury and fame.   60
Blest souls ! the happiest of their kind, who knew
The primal good, and had the sense to live.
Pleased in the humble sphere that God assigned.
Yet not unchequer'd was their course of life.
Clouds mix'd with sunshine, oft would intervene;   65
Failure of health, or some domestic flaw
Ruffled the even current of their days ;
Or some disaster sudden, unforseen,

Caused agitation in the little state.

So it fell out, when Aubrey, luckless wight,   70

At Guerrick* got embroil'd about this time ;

And wrathful at the jade who stole his watch

Had dragg'd her to the magisterial bench.

Not fortunate like Judah, he had none,

No kind Adullamite, no friend so sure   75

To send for watch or pledge : but blind with rage,

He charged the wretched girl, and thus reveal'd

His folly, and his sin thus found him out.

Yet nothing of the deed was heard or known

Among the Lindsey folk : so quiet all,   80

So calm, contented, with but knowledge scant

Of all the outside world, lived they unmoved :

Until their minister, who rarely sought

Police reports, by providence had seen

A notice of this strange untoward affair   85

Duly recorded in provincial news.

Old Aubrey's wife much wonder'd why her man

Should go to Guerrick twice in the same week,

Nor valued much the reasons that he gave.

Shock'd was Nortonio when he read the tale,   90

And re-read, scarcely crediting his eyes ;

* See Glossary,

But there it was in all its ugliness,
A record foul of folly and of guilt:
Rendered more hateful by the glaring fact,
That what led to inquiry had been done   95
The day before, when he as parish clerk
Had taken part in that most holy rite
Commemorative of the Saviour's death.
The crime was one week old, when first it caught
The wondering parson's eye. Deep was his grief: 100
Horror and black vexation rack'd his mind.
The Lord's day follow'd with the rising sun,
And quick dismissal of the unseemly clerk
Was peremptory.—Time there was not left
Clardonis to consult, then distant far.   105
Much did he ponder—With the early dawn
He sought his friend the Warden Possumus
And opened all his troubles in detail.
Stagger'd was he to hear such dreadful news
Of one who long a faithful slave had been,   110
And recently obtained a prize conferr'd
For length of service and a just career.
Amazement for a moment held him mute.
Not more astonished is the antler'd hart,   •
When wondering at the approach of horrid sounds, 115

Roused from his lair, he hears the yelling pack
And bounds impetuous through the crackling brake.
Words found at last a vent, and honest rage
Commutual fired the warden and his priest.
Prompt was the declaration : now no more   120
Clerk of dear Lindsey should that Aubrey be.
Grieved if he were the bishop he might seek,
If more he wanted in the courts of law.
But Snap should take his place in church that day.
And if approved before seven days had run,   125
With sanction of the vicar be install'd
And charged with all the duties of that post.
Busier than usual on that solemn day
Were Lindsey tongues.   Swift flew the rumour round
From house to house : but bit by bit at first   130
The horrible discovery was made.
At length it reached his own dear cottage, once
The scene of peace and homeborn happiness ;
Bereft of all the dread arena now,
The theatre of strife, contention dire !   135
Age all forgotten, fiery eyes and tongues
Flaming with vengence vollied forth a storm
Of passion unrestrain'd.   Weakness no more
Withheld the wife, though crippled in both legs.

Fierce from her chair she sprang : Grasp'd with   140
Both hands the besom stale that lay beside the door,
And in a corner caught her guilty spouse.
There she and her old sister, prompt to help,
From quiet souls both into furies changed,
Belabour'd the poor wretch, till shrieks of woe   145
Resounded through the neighbourhood, and told
The sad effects of wicked thoughts and sin.

    Stung with disgust the first time since he knew
The place, Nortonio turn'd his back and sought
Eric's abode, called Curlieu, not remote   150
From Lindsey church, an easy evening walk.
There piety and elegance combined
To soften human cares and shed a charm
O'er all the changes that each day brought forth.
There in the loved society of those   155
He valued for their virtues, comfort sure
Nortonio found, and could his thoughts disclose
In perfect safety without fear of guile.
The ladies of that house with lovely tact
Brighten'd the darkest hour, nor suffer'd gloom   160
And melancholy to absorb the soul.
There grateful as the smell of new-mown hay
And sweet as fragrance from the jess'mine bowers

At summer eve, their observations fell,

Well-timed, well-tempered, seasonable, pure,   165

And duly weighted with a modest fear,

That much there might be yet unknown to them :

What e'er their subject never press'd too far.

To that abode of harmony and love,

Sure of a welcome by his generous friend,   170

Could time be spared, the parson oft would go

And pick up local knowledge and advice.

Thither he turn'd his steps, and seated soon

Began the converse, and shook from his mind

The hateful burden of the Lindsey clerk,   175

And made but slight allusion though he saw

By signs infallible that all was known.

They talk'd of Hattham* and the changes there,

The frequent changes, that had taken place

Since he, the prince of Grecian scholars, ruled   180

The neighbouring parish and lord paramount

Of learned oracles awed country squires.

Mighty was he in word if not in deed.

Due homage from the sons of trade he gained

In all the midland parts, who deem'd their homes   185

Honour'd by banquets, where this tasteful clerk

---

* See Glossary.

Partook of sucking pig and puff'd his smoke.
The smoke had vanish'd and the learning too,
When some years later, on the coach outside
Travelling from Guerrick to the Midland mart,   190
Nortonio pointing to that domicile,
Where once the hero of the schools abode,
Call'd to his comrade on the coach and said,
" There lived the mighty Parr, the famous man."
Alas! the traveller nothing knew of Greek,   195
And pondering on the fame of Parr, exclaim'd
" Old Parr! Parr's pills are famous pills indeed!
Amused was Eric with the strange mistake,
Proof of the vanity of high renown
In ancient languages and classic lore.   200
" Still was his fame as good," exclaim'd the wife,
" As that of the young poet, who admired
" In distant parts, left where he once had dwelt
But one memorial, that an unpaid debt:
A debt so trivial, that it had escaped   205
The debtor's memory, but still remain'd
Long due and vivid, in the tradesman's mind.
Time cut the conversation short, for night
Drew nigh: and hast'ning through the dark'ning road
The parson sought his home and breathed awhile   210

Free from his village cares, but mortified
And humbled that his mission proved so vain.

Now changes came apace : some grown in years
And some in ailments, dying, breaches made,
In such a population, sad and great.   215

Say ye, who know the causes of all things
In this material world, who shrewdly prove
The secrets of sly nature, and can show
How many million years must intervene
Between the present and the past, before   220
The layers and strata of this puzzling earth
Had form'd their dark deposits and proclaim'd
The world much older than the Scriptures tell,
Say, ye philosophers, the reason why
Births, deaths, and marriages in clusters come.   225
In prosperous days and in a populous town
When wealth flows in, young couples wisely seize
The joyous time and enter on their bliss.
Like causes all urge on : example spreads   ·
Contagious : and the reasons we can tell.   230
If neighbours too who have grown old together
Should die at the same time, needs not surprise.
But in a little calm community,
Where every day but the reflection is

Of what was yesterday, and knows no change   235
Of poverty or riches, and the folk
Not subject to those influences exist,
Strange is it that the same rule should prevail.
Calvus, a new inhabitant but old,
Ten years beyond the three score years and ten   240
Had seen, and still with martial ardour glow'd.
To walk to Guerrick from his village home
And thence walk back he but a trifle deem'd,
Though younger men a seven mile walk eschew'd.
This feat he dared, accomplish'd and retired   245
To bed as usual : thence he ne'er arose
In health again, but breathed away his soul
Calm and confiding in his Saviour's love.
Vain had it been to tell the aged man,
That youth no more was his; his strength no more 250
Could bear such labours. Still he fondly clung
To long-form'd habits and his ancient boast,
That with his regiment he could march full-arm'd
Without fatigue and camp himself at night.
No bed of sickness his : mere o'er-wrought strength 255
And nature tax'd beyond its proper powers
Failing succumb'd to an unwise attempt.
The close was sudden, unforeseen by all,

The neighbours, children, doctor, or the priest,
So hale and jovial had the veteran been.   260
His children were at hand and did their part :
No stranger nurse embitter'd his last hour.
His daughter, Calva, faithful to the last
With filial piety supplied his wants,
Consoled his languid limbs, eased the fatigue   265
That press'd his worn-out frame, and turn'd his thoughts
To brighter worlds and pointed to that hope
Given to believers in their blessed Lord.
   Soon follow'd from this ever changing scene
One whose lot was far different, Homo's wife,   270
A loving mother and a helpmate true,
Honest, industrious, kind to all around.
Slowly the malady had wrought its way
And given her notice that this world no more
Must be her resting place : that soon her child   275
And husband must be left to toil alone.
With meek submission to the Saviour's will
She gave up all and turn'd her thoughts entire
To preparation for a future world.
Dear to Nortonio was this child of God,   280
Though rear'd and nurtured in a place least fit
As some would think, e'en in a village inn.

Oft to that place the parson turn'd his course,
And in the chamber where the sufferer lay,
Sore tried by mortal throes a welcome found.   285
A willing listener on that bed of pain
Join'd in his prayers and fervently replied
To all his exhortations, nor e'er deem'd
That of the Gospel she could hear enough.
Oh ! there were two or three who really felt   290
That He was with them, that the word divine
To those who met and worshipp'd in His name
Was then fulfill'd.   The world and all its gear
Was banish'd for a time from all their minds;
Whilst in the interval from suffering snatch'd   295
Their much-loved minister raised high their thoughts
From earth to heaven, from holiness to God.
Sweet was the pastor's work when thus engaged,
When such a blest occasion he enjoyed,
And to congenial spirits could unfold   300
The mighty wonders of redeeming love.
Sweet too to such to read those psalms inspired,
Th' immortal labours of the Hebrew king,
Who found in piety that peace of mind
He vainly sought in empire or in pomp.   305
There in that humble room, all unadorn'd

But barely furnish'd, rustic, clean and neat,
Those sacred songs that comforted of old
The children of their God on Zion's hill
Fell like the dew of heaven on English hearts.   310
There it was their delight, supreme delight,
To priest and people to ignore the world,
To join in sweet communion, to converse
And tell what great things had been done for them
By God the Father, Son, and Holy Ghost.   315
What matter'd it to them, the world knew not,
The world could not appreciate joys like theirs!
And so Nortonio left his Christian friend
In Jesus' hands, her firm, her only hope;
And He received her.   Calm her spirit pass'd.   320
The body worn with suffering peaceful lay
Prepared to pay the penalty of sin.
This living friends interr'd, and tears sincere
As ever issued from a human eye
Were shed on that occasion.   But they thank'd   325
God who had taken to Himself the soul
Of their departed sister: gain to her,
Loss to survivors!   None more truly mourn'd
Though full of thankfulness and joy serene,
Than did their pastor.   To his cottage room,   330

E   59

Where temporary rest he sometimes found,
In haste he sped, and there in solitude
Wept bitterly—wept that the sins of men
Had brought into this world such scenes of death,
Such separations from the dearest friends,   335
Such deep humiliation, such disgrace
E'en to that being who at first was form'd
In likeness of his God. 'Twas all in vain!
Dead on account of sin the body is.
No tears that men can shed can wash the stain   340
That sin has made. Thanks then be to our God
For that supreme unutterable gift—
The gift of a Redeemer! One, whose power
Both sin and death have felt and Satan too,
Who vanquish'd lies beneath His conquering arm.   345
    Now death and sickness dogg'd his steps so close,
That not unwillingly Nortonio turn'd,
When call'd to bear a share in others' woes
And visit neighbouring parishes, where aid
Was sought for public or for private ends.   350
A loving union still prevail'd between
Nortonio and his time-tried Clarebrook friends :
On his side gratitude, on theirs respect
And love and faithfulness, remembrance sweet

Of many conversations they enjoyed,   355
And hints and kind suggestions all well-timed.
So in their troubles still they look'd to him,
As friend and neighbour, as a man who lived
Not for his own alone, but others' good.
The brother of old Possumus lived there,   360
And still the farm he held in former days,
When Woven was his landlord, he retain'd.
And now a malady whose fatal end
Sound science could foretell, had seized his wife.
She was a woman in whose loyal heart   365
Her husband could confide : his happiness
For time and for eternity she sought.
All other subjects held a second place
Save love to God and faith in Jesus Christ.
Well did she look to all her household's ways—   370
Active by day, and vigilant by night.
No lazy servant maids or lads uncouth
Found comfort there : unwarn'd they fled the place,
And saw with ready instinct in that house
Where such a mistress ruled, no home for them.   375
Good did she to her husband all her days,
And sent him forth good humour'd to his toil,
Early each morning, e're the sun suck'd up

The dew-drop twinkling on the mountain side.
Well was he known too in the county hall,   380
When as a juryman he took his place,
And sat among the elders of the land,
Clean and well-dress'd, respectable not prim,
A sample of what honest men should be.
When to his house he came four goodly sons   385
Rose up to do his pleasure; such they knew
Was mother's wish, their first care and delight:
And close at hand to welcome back her sire
The daughter stood, prepared with smiles to greet
And by her love anticipate each wish.   390
Such was his happy home, and such he knew
He owed all under God to her now sick.
Deep anguish struck into his inmost soul
When first he heard the terrible report,
That she, the partner of his joys and cares,   295
Must quit ere long this worldly scene, no more
Be seen in those loved rooms, where hitherto
All things had moved in harmony with her.
And great was her distress when first she knew
That ere some months had passed she must depart,   400
Must quit all that had charm'd her on her way
In this world, husband, home, and children dear.

Some terrors too beset that loving heart,
When first she thought on death's dark valley nigh,
Though regular in all her duties, loved   405
By God and man, in charity with all.
She felt herself a sinner far removed
From what a perfect child of God should be:
And so she trembled, when she look'd beyond
The limits of this world and faintly saw   410
The awful matters of eternity—
She loved her bible: o'er its pages pored
And honour'd much the Church and minister:
But still some yearning to remain and see
Her family still prosperous held her soul: 415
Whilst meditating on the sad result
She shrank with some misgivings from the change.
Most opportune then was Nortonio's call,
Who reason'd gently and brought back her mind
Into a tranquil state, serene, resign'd   420
To God's most holy will. That He alone
Knew what was best: that whatsoe're He will'd
Must wisdom be. Her old friend fix'd her thoughts
On that blest Book, which always in the prime
Of health was her delight, and there she found,   425
If it were good in the eternal eye,

Like Lazarus and Dives friends should see
And know each other : therefore husband dear,
And children much beloved, might meet again
In that mysterious world, where they who loved   430
Their God above all beings, should enjoy
What ear hath never heard, nor eye hath seen,
Nor heart conceived.   And as for proper times,
The time when to be born, the time to die,
Lay far beyond the ken of human wit.   435
Cheer'd was the godly woman : quickly she
Recover'd all her usual peace of mind,
And view'd the approaching crisis, calm prepared
To meet her God and give up earth for heaven.

    Next Wolverdingtre claim'd Nortonio's care.   440
Deep in a quiet dell it lay, obscure,
But little known, close to the Lindsey bounds.
The pastor of that small and lovely spot
Press'd by his private matters was well pleased
To have such help as then Nortonio gave.   445
And there he found fresh objects to arrest
His pity and attention, and receive
Drops of sweet solace from the word of God.
There a poor soul he found, whose shattered frame
Was rack'd with pains rheumatic, shrunk and bent : 450

And yet with honest industry he strove
To earn a livelihood : and since his legs
Were powerless now their office to perform,
He sat as schoolmaster to teach the swains
Their alphabet and some arithmetic.   455
He had been famous in his day to draw
Long drains beneath the clayey soil, and judge
Where best superfluous moisture might exude :
But now the sad results of such a damp
Unhealthy occupation supervened.   460
The little knowledge at a Sunday school
Gain'd years ago was now most dearly prized,
And made him useful to his friends around.
The farmers, glad to keep their rates all free
From such a burden, fail'd not to support   465
And help him forward in his good design.
In that diseased body dwelt a mind
Still active, independent, anxious too
His fellow creatures to improve and aid ;
A mind which had it known the genial rays   470
Of science, might have led the sons of wealth
Through undiscover'd realms of art and skill.
Close by in perfect contrast dwelt a clown,
The village blacksmith, rough, uncouth, untamed,

Sordid and selfish. Worthy of the stem   475
From which they sprang his children had grown up,
A son and daughter. She now distant lived
In service. Troublesome reports had reac h'd
The father, caring little, but compell'd
To fetch her home, for charges were alleged   480
Impugning her integrity, and she
Recriminated by a charge most foul
Against her master's son. In hurried haste
Forthwith her brother to the rescue flew,
And brought her home without a day's delay.   485
Ill she arrived, for she had fallen sick
Just when suspicions of the missing things
Cluster'd about her like a swarm of bees.
No time was lost in seeking parish aid
And gifts of money from the rich around,   490
Though funds sufficient for his daily wants,
And large allowance for his alehouse freaks,
The blacksmith's trade had yielded. Such a chance
Was not to be neglected. Loud the cry,
The vicar was away, and he, who now   495
Acted as substitute, was dull and slow
Want to anticipate where none should be.
A fussy magistrate who in his zeal

To rise to notice would officious be,
Caught up the cry, and thus became a tool   500
In their designing hands, though every need
Of soul and body was at once supplied.
The girl lay ill; but what was her complaint
The surgeon would not or he could not tell.
Ere many days the son himself fell sick   505
And soon he died : and dying, said he caught
His ailment from his sister. She still lived,
Nor suffered much from weakness or from pain,
So long as goodly fare abundant came
From richer neighbours or the Union Board.   510
Dirt, discontent, and gloomy looks around
Pervaded that drear dwelling ; absent all
Attempts at cleanliness : and piety
In such a climate it was hard to find.
     Near stood a cottage where at that time lay   515
A poor young creature just upon the verge
Of womanhood, whose hectic cheek and face
And form attenuated plainly show'd
That in her budding youth her strength was gone.
And yet contentment sat upon her face,   520
Calm resignation and a placid frame
Of mind composed and patiently prepared

To bear whatever burden hers might be.
The kind good daughter of a farmer near,
A few years older, tended her with care 525
And watching every symptom, minister'd
To all her wants, as one with her in Christ,
Smoothing her pillow with a sister's love.
Glad was Nortonio to behold the girl
So good and so afflicted, cherish'd thus 530
By such a saintly soul, for leave he must:
His warden Possumus required his care,
A sudden malady his frame had seized
And clogg'd the action of those parts within
By which alone his body could exist 535
In health and strength; yet cheerful he held up
His venerable head, and rosy still,
But streak'd with suffering, his good tempered face
Turn'd with a pleasant smile on all around.
The best and most judicious, who excell'd 540
In healing arts, to his assistance came
But came in vain. Short was the interview
Between the pastor and his much-loved friend.
The doctor's orders and good sense forbade
Much conversation. So Nortonio closed 345
With little reading and a few brief prayers,

And left the worthy warden to his God,
With grave misgivings that his death was nigh,
A sad presentiment that proved too true.

    Nor yet unnoticed was Nortonio's toil.   550
More than one benefice had he declined.
His quiet course he held, combining both
The care of pupils and a rural charge.
But now a godly man had gone to rest
And left his flock forlorn without a guide.   555
Press'd was the Patron : with hot haste a swarm
Of hungry candidates beset his path,
And urged their claims to fill the vacant post.
But he, grown old and wary, paused awhile,
Took time to think and check'd the clamorous tribe. 560
Of scholarship some notion he could form,
Not far from a correct one : but their hearts
He could not dive into : so counsel sought
From reverend neighbours known through many years.
The income of the living was but small,   565
And yet a pastor to befriend the poor
Was sadly needed. With becoming care
The patron look'd around and sought advice.
Consulting with his neighbours soon he found
That what was wanted was a man of sense,   570

Kind-hearted, pious, one who would reside
Upon the spot and tend the little flock.
The vicarage for years in ruin lay ;
The pastor living in the mansion-house
He rented from the squire ; and thence arose   575
A difficulty : means small, but expense
Not light, to keep up usages begun.
His reverend friends unhesitating told
The patron that Nortonio was the man
To hold this cure of souls, if but inclined   580
To live as did the last priest in that house.
The hint was taken and the offer made.
And so Nortonio after guidance sought
Low at the throne of grace, from wisdom's fount
Infallible, this new charge undertook.   585

END OF CANTO III.

PART II.

INTRODUCTION.

PLACED in a world of wonders from his birth,
   Man sees but little of its real worth.
Incessant changes crowd life's narrow span,
Changes no mortal can foresee or plan.
Youth treads on childhood, manhood follows fast,   5
Before of follies he has seen the last.
Then schemes unnumber'd tantalize the brain,
Till age steps in and shows all cares but vain.
In Eden's holy shades there might be rest
And love, the daily portion of the blest.   10
But strife and change and troubles undefined
Fill'd up the curse on Adam and his kind.
Whilst human life in centuries was told
Some schemes enduring human minds could hold.
Great power did he possess o'er young compeers   15
Who counted birthdays through nine hundred years.

The rising spirit of grim discontent
Scarce dared to show itself or find a vent.
Succeeding generations view'd with awe
Their sire and priest, and deem'd his will their law.　20
But sin had enter'd and its wages death
And the earth quaked the horrid scourge beneath.
The spirit of unrest had found a stage
On which to revel and to glut its rage.
Though for a season it was held at bay,　　　　25
It broke at last o'er patriarchal sway ;
Made of the human brain a fruitful mine
To carry out its own insane design.
The apple of contention Satan hurl'd
Among the tenants of the seething world,　　　30
And saw with hellish joy the human race
Bring on themselves both ruin and disgrace.
From bad to worse the worthless creatures sank,
Till all around with deep corruption stank.
Excesses, violence and utter scorn　　　　　35
Of right and justice seized the woman-born.
God saw th' ungrateful wretch His love despise
And bade the Deluge o'er his revels rise.
One only family remain'd to tell
How with the righteous God would deign to dwell.　40

Then life was shorten'd : as the days of man
Decreased in number, rapid change began :
Change in the world of nature, change in food,
Change in the habits both of bad and good.
This soon was seen ; and to o'ercome the power   45
Of time and change th' ambitious built a tower,
A tower to be with its great top sublime
A centre of endurance through all time,
Forgetful that the Lord if He incline
Could with a breath disperse their grand design.   50
Then war and slaughter, blood-shed without end
In quick succession on their steps attend.
Red through the annals of four thousand years,
The tale of murder, scarcely check'd, appears.
Change then became a source of health and joy,   55
Means which the God of wisdom would employ.
Stagnation in the social state had been
As great a bane, as if the world marine,
Void of health-bearing gales and tides had stood,
One vast, one motionless and noisome flood.   60
On much-loved subjects still the mind would dwell,
And fondly deem in such no change were well.
So thought the Roman ruler,* when he gave
Most pressing orders to his trusty slave,

* Vespasian.

That not a plant or tree or stone or wall   65
Should change its place or alter'd be, of all
That form'd the nursery of his early days,
The scene of boyhood that he loved to praise.
How pleased beholds the veteran of fourscore
The fields that strong in youth he bounded o'er;   70
Views every tree, examines every nook
And scarce can satisfy his loving look.
Change then must be our lot, whilst here we wait
A mightier change, that brings us to a state,
Which, whatsoe'er it be, we know is rest,   75
If by God's grace we be among the blest.

CANTO IV.

CANTO IV.

Years multitudinous had roll'd away,
Deep buried in the vortex of the past,
When in that church-yard on the Lindsey height
Nortonio stood, and far and wide surveyed
The lovely landscape, whilst across his mind   5
Shot vivid images of times gone by.
Not far off in the valley spread below,
Just seen above the tops of tufted trees,
A little church-spire twinkled in the sun ;
While lost in thought he scann'd the well-known
    scene,   10
New was this object.   Soon he recognized
The site of Clarebrook, and recall'd to mind
The rumours at a distance he had heard :
How filial piety a solace sought,
How the loved child enshrined the dear remains   15
Of a fond father, and with wealth untold
Bade the best architect with all his taste
Rear on that spot a gem-like church to God.
Then glanced his eye upon the mansion front
That whiten'd in the distance, where endear'd   20

By acts of charity and sympathy
With all, the Widow and the Daughter dwelt.
Bathed in a flood of light, for then the sun
Career'd in dazzling splendour, nature round
Reposed, complacent in the Sabbath calm.   25
Sweet were the rapid moments, whilst he mused
And gazed delighted on the different points
That caught his eye, and quickly brought again
Back to remembrance friends both old and dear.
Spread like an amphitheatre the scene   30
Before him lay, embracing far and wide
Spots where his lot had been to minister
Or sojourn.   Far upon the utmost verge
That eye could reach peer'd up the hazy heights
Of Edgehill, noted for the strife of Charles   35
And Lindsay's bloody relics, still preserved
With selfish care, memorials of the fray.
Not far off lay the fields, but dimly seen,
If seen at all, where once as beneficed
He lived, and blessing others bless'd himself.   40
Much did he muse upon the days gone by,
And a long list of dear parishioners
Rose quick into his mind and pictured forth
Sweet visions of the past, where love to God

And love to man had cheer'd this vale of tears.   45
Then turn'd his eye upon the Garden-Town
Where dimly rising slow the smoke appear'd,
And fringed th' horizon with a sable cloud.
There rested long his thoughts: much he recall'd
Of sin, of folly, piety and pride;   50
How Irish parsons penniless and proud
Work'd on weak women, and beneath the cloak
Of zeal religious schemed for selfish ends.
In contrast with the beauteous scene around,
And black with envy for the heavenly calm   55
That rested for a moment on the world,
The evil spirit seem'd to hover near,
And bring into his mind a train of thoughts,
Retracing rapidly a hideous list
Of pious quacks and self-deceiving fools.   60
But there stood forth amidst the misty crowd
That throng'd his mind, some few, some godly souls,
That sought the praise of God, not praise of man.
Long had he mused, and longer still had stayed
And fed on recollections of the past,   65
Had not his friend Promnens impatient grown,
And, sallying from his domicile, cut short
The parson's meditations too prolong'd.

73

"Good Sir, you're long in coming : I and friends
Await you with a welcome," thus exclaim'd   70
The farmer, "in my old and well-known home."
He spake, and with a cordial shake of hands
Hurried his friend along the garden-walk
That led them to his hospitable door.
Then entering in Nortonio welcome found   75
Sincere and hearty from his Lindsey friends
That met beneath the roof-tree of his host.
The mistress of that family he learn'd
Had died long since, and now another friend—
The sister of his host—presided there :   80
No stranger to him, for in former times
She with her brother lived on Blacon top.
The sons were grown to manhood, whom he hail'd
As boys when last he saw them, now become
Two sprightly youths, well-form'd, and ardent both 85
In horsemanship and yeomanry pursuits
To show their skill and challenge future fame.
Barbats his brother and his sister now,
The widow of poor Amnes long deceased,
Were close at hand to welcome back their friend,   90
For as their pastor he had not yet come,
But simply to fill up a void then caused

74

By illness of the usual minister.

Steaming with balmy heat and simmering sighs

A mighty tea-pot of the ancient school   95

Stood on the table, promising to all

Refreshing beverage good for head and soul.

Rich currant cake and jams whose odours sweet

Charm'd the guest's nose, were spread around
> the board,

Thick interspersed with plates of home-made bread 100

Cut into slices and with butter clad,

The bread and butter pure without alloy.

Such were the friends, and such the fragrant meal

Nortonio now was summoned to partake.

Soon finish'd was all eating : drain'd were cups   105

Of dark decoction from the Chinese plant

Well-sweeten'd, mantled with a coat of cream,

Such as an honest dairy only yields,

All innocent of city wiles and art ;

While pleasing conversation fill'd each void.   110

Many and pregnant were the questions ask'd

And answers promptly given by guest and host ;

But broken, unconnected was discourse,

Till tea-urn, tea-tray, apparatus all

Had been removed, and in their place disposed   115

Full canisters of cakes and fruits well-dried,
With bright decanters shining in the sun,
Well-fill'd with home-made wines, dark elderberry
And amber cowslip, sight indeed to some,
Blest with a strong digestion and hale health,   120
Acceptable, but to their guest that day
A source of secret horror, for he knew
Such sweets, if taken, would but prove to him
The sad forerunners of stomachic woe.

Impatient grew Nortonio to acquire   125
Some certain knowledge of the state of things
That had existed since he left the place.
The death of dear Clardonis, and the change
In Wardenship that follow'd the decease
Of Possumus, were things well-known to him ;   130
But still he wish'd particulars to learn,
And press'd his friend Promnens to tell the whole.
Two glasses of old cowslip cheer'd his heart,
And then with modest accent he began.

" When first you left us sorrowing to assume   135
The charge that we supposed would be the last,
And occupy your thoughts as long as life
Was spared, from different parts came ministers,
Who with the Vicar's help the duty took,

As well as circumstances would permit.   140
Soon happily our church the notice gain'd
Of wealthy neighbours; one himself a priest,
Who with his wife, a godly woman too,
Purchased the mansion, where in times gone by
Your presence oft was seen, and he became   145
As it was thought Perpetual Curate here.
Possess'd of ample means and cultured taste
And free to follow all their good designs,
They lost no time in planning various schemes
For spending money.   First it was their care   150
The mansion to enlarge, erect a lodge,
Stables construct, and beautify the grounds.
But whilst thus busy in their own affairs,
Forward they were to help our little church,
Pull down the rotten pews and in their place   155
Put up new seats, well-season'd, clean, and dry.
Our worthy vicar cordially concurr'd.
He and the new-arrived, good Protestants,
Were zealous in Church matters; thought the same
About Church doctrines; and repell'd with scorn   160
The novelties and innovations vain,
Such as we hear have stealthily crept in,
And discord bred in parishes elsewhere.

Thus fortunate we deem'd our lot, rejoiced
And thankful felt for such a happy state.   165
Not many months had pass'd ere discord rose,
And quarrels about pews, the dry old bone
Of bitter strife, contested all in vain.
Our late good Warden's nephew had arranged
That where his uncle lived, his foreman now   170
Should dwell, and overlook the farm for him :
The pew, that had been to that house assign'd
For years, he claim'd, and bade his children there
Sit at the time of worship, which annoyed
Our minister's good lady, who had claim'd   175
This for her own especial use, and deem'd
What she had done had given a right
To choose before all others, but our swains,
As you well know, to all dictation deaf,
Spurn'd the idea, and I grieve to add   180
Resisted the attempt with insolence.
Then both withdrew offended : I was grieved,
And thought that better temper and respect
Our people should have shown to those who sought
To do them good and little interfere.   185
Another minister was soon obtain'd ;
And we were left with the remains of strife,

And a church newly pew'd and well arranged.
But soon the vicar died, and then a change
Took place more sweeping : new plans introduced, 190
The people call'd on to bestir themselves,
Shake off old habits, grasp ideas fresh,
And keep pace with the spirit of the times.
But meanwhile changes in the ways and views
Of worship, foreign to our church and rule, 195
Had silently crept in and undermined
That harmony and peace that once prevail'd
In this our village. Rank and rapid grew
This upstart doctrine, like some new-thrown seed
Of swede or mangold from a distance brought, 200
Cast by the sower on ground well prepared.
Some who had humbly come before to learn,
Now boldly and officiously held up
Their empty heads, to teach and to explain
What they themselves could never comprehend. 205
Fervour, fanatic zeal and violence,
Coarse language, nasal twang and sour grimace,
Usurped the place of humble piety.
With all their cant much I incline to think
Some were sincere and wished to serve their God. 210
One far beyond the rest was prominent,

And gave a proof that he did. He avouch'd
And argued well that if a soul were saved
'T were worth a whole life's labour. He was right!
But much I fear that ere a soul was saved,   215
Evils innum'rable had enter'd in,
Seized many a soul and covered it with guile,
Pride, ignorance, assurance without ground,
Which they call faith, these ate into their heart
As rust eats into iron. Still that man   220
Of whom I spoke, well by his conduct show'd
That what he sought was glory to his God.
Well nigh had he contrived to have a piece
Of land conveyed in all due legal style,
And bought, henceforth to be the future site   225
Of a new meeting-house, a thing unknown
In our calm village, had not Anakson
With his shrewd usual foresight intervened,
And quietly convinced him that such deed
Would lead to discord : hitherto much strife   230
Had not been known amongst us, and the worst
Of bickering and contention was indeed
Religious strife. He show'd himself alive
To common sense, expostulation calm,
And dropp'd the dear design. I must confess   235

That in the doings of our neighbour now
I did concur: though Anakson and I
In almost all things else opposed each other.
This agitation, these dissenting schemes
Began some years before, and I opine   240
Neglect of the commandment number Five
Was the true cause. Our children first begin
To set us at defiance; servants then
Are quick to follow bad example set,
And so at last all order and all rule   245
In matters holy and things temporal
Are thought of little moment, till at last
The world a scene of wild confusion seems.
No doubt whatever the Arch-fiend himself
Was at the bottom of this hated change.   250
Our present vicar when he came and found
Things so unsettled, tried with gentle hand
To stay the evil, and the canting tribe
To lead into the church; but found he might
As well have tried an adder to subdue   255
And bid him fondly with his children play.
Most energetic he appears to be
In missionary efforts, and in all
The objects that Societies design

Which love the Bible and the truth of God.   260
Good is what he desires, and well deserves
His name Philagathus.   It had been well,
If with a weighty hand he had suppress'd
The rising evil : crush'd its head at once,
As you once taught us to crush nettle tops.   265
I bode no good among our labouring class
From this mistaken zeal.   Bishops and priests
Of all men should teach order and stop strife.
Reflections have I heard oft freely thrown
On former parsons, but the priests of old   270
Were gentlemen and men of honour too,
Who to their doctrines stuck, turn'd not about
To all points of the compass, just as whim
Or interest or popular applause
Dictated, and with less profession too   275
Were quite as pious as the modern race.
Witness how true religion, reverence due
To God Almghty enter'd into deeds
That public were consider'd.   Common wills
And e'en th' indentures that in duty bound   280
The parish 'prentice to his master's trade
Proclaim'd to all the providence of God.
But now in these free-thinking times the name

Of God is oft omitted : that of man
Put forward as if he alone were lord,   285
And all the universe must yield to him."

    He spake and paused ; for now he saw full well
His reverend friend was weary grown, to hear
Such tedious details, such unhoped complaints.
Silence was quickly broken : sundry thoughts   290
Found utterance in the circle. Sage remark
Pass'd rapidly with solemn emphasis
As well became so deep a theme discuss'd.
All were agreed that they should like to know
The chief points in Nortonio's late career.   295
And unmistakably gave him to see
That such was their desire, who thus replied :
" Dear friends and worthy neighbours, dear to me
For many reasons which I will not state :
Thus in your presence it is best to be.   300
For years you know that I resided near,
Incumbent of a parish not far hence,
And heard oft of your doings, till at length
Impell'd by conscience and a strong desire
To serve the Lord more fully, I resign'd   305
The living and prepared for other scenes.
But to the patron first I notice gave

One year before, that to resign the post
Was my intention.   Thus he had the time
To choose a good successor, which design,   310
At his request, I help'd him to effect.
Unwillingly I left the place, but felt
That I must leave then, if I left at all :
That e'en delays but for some few years more
Would bar all future change, that rooted then   315
And bound by stronger ties, advanced in years
Change to another scene I must forego.
So with the patron we a parson chose :
And chose the fittest man, uninfluenced
By family connexions, or the claims   320
Of pushing friends or private selfish schemes.
Free then to rove I and my careworn wife,
Who in my labours always took her share,
As well you know, thought that occasion fair
To give ourselves a holiday, and see   325
Lands sever'd from us by that silver streak
Which some have deem'd the safeguard of our land.
To wealthy capitals we made our way,
And there beheld with mingled grief and joy
Endless experiments of human pride,   330
Innumerable scenes of vanity.

Pomp, splendour, gorgeous show, dire poverty
Met in close contrast, form'd a medley strange,
On which the mind of man might ponder long.
Close to the walls of huge cathedrals, built   335
In grandest style, where wealth and art superb
Had spent their utmost powers, we often found
A wretched crowd of human beings, sunk
In filth, half-starved, half-naked and half-housed.
The smells were horrible! how different far   340
From the fresh breeze we catch upon this hill!
One good effect of travel is to make
The heart content with what it finds at home.
Not that I think that capitals abroad
Are worse than our own London, or afford,   345
Except in some few points, more cause to mourn.
Where human beings congregate in crowds
Vice seems inherent in our present state :
However crush'd it struggles on, at times
Rises defiant, or creeps undiscern'd,   350
But like a snake behind it leaves a trail.
Intemp'rance here holds riot, drunkenness
Stinks at the corner ; fraud and avarice
In ambush lie, th' unwary to entrap.
But forms acknowledged of licentiousness   355

Which sanction'd are by laws in foreign parts
In London are not legal.   Bigotry
Is there more rarely seen.   The danger is
That too much freedom is allow'd to those
Who arrogate the right to judge of creeds.   360
Our Romish brethren on the continent
Are not all devotees : indifferent some,
Or deem religion a mere tool of state.
But most are kind and hospitable, like
Our Romish neighbours here, whose hearts enlarged 365
And free from narrow views deserve all praise.
In sculpture and in painting foreign hands
Excel our own.   Their galleries and halls
Free from the venal fee ope wide their doors,
And greet with courtesy the visitor.   370
But the great charm that makes a British home
Is there not seen.   The Bible, that blest book,
That sits in state upon the cottage shelf
And consecrates the lowliest English house,
Is there but rarely found.   Domestic sweets,   375
Such as in England bind us to the spot,
Seem little valued.   Show and vain parade
And public pleasure most attention gain.
God's holy day, which every pious soul

Loves here to honour, there is oft profaned 380
By greed of trade or folly's vain pursuits.
Oft on our way to worship on that day
We pass'd by scenes of vanity and vice,
Mix'd up with symbols and strange spectacles
Of slavish superstition and blind faith. 385
One man I saw stretch'd prostrate on the flags
Absorb'd in deep devotion, crouch'd before
A senseless image fasten'd in the wall.
So earnest was he that he ne'er perceived
Me, the spectator, though I gazed some time. 390
In person as to make and frame most like
Yourself, good Promnens, was this man devote ;
In mind far different as we all well know.
When with our friends we traversed Waterloo
And view'd the plains where Gaul and Briton join'd 395
In mortal strife, at Hougomout we found
An image of the Virgin placed aloft,
The toes of which had been but slightly scorch'd,
Ere our brave guards the conflagration quench'd.
With shot and shell the French that post assail'd 400
And fired the chapel, but our men repell'd
All their assaults, and crush'd the rising flame,
The zealous Belgians pointed out to us

How shrank the fire before the Virgin form,
Not daring more, although the toes were caught.   405
Right glad were we to turn our steps and hail
Far in the distance once more Albion's cliffs
And sojourn for a time in Brighton town.
Thence to the huge metropolis we went.
There long we had not stayed ere offers came   410
And invitations to accept a charge
E'en in this county and not far from hence.
The call I follow'd.   There my stay was short.
The people grateful far too highly prized
My labours for them brief but profitable;   415
The schools got into order, and a piece
Of land was added to their burial ground,
Which years before they vainly strove to gain.
And when I left, they did not let me leave
Without substantial proof of their esteem.   420
Thence to the north we turn'd and there abode,
Charged with a mission in a busy place,
Throng'd with a population dense and coarse.
Clever, industrious, strong, inured to toil,
The people labour'd in the dirtiest trades   425
And earn'd enormous wages: then consumed
Their profits in intemperance and vice.

As usual all the penalties of sin
They had to pay. Disease in hideous forms
Struck down their strength, made them reluctant
   think,   430
And ponder on the folly of their lives.
Judge what a change to me from these fair scenes.
So rough in their appearance, so uncouth
The people were, that my poor wife was scared
And scarcely ventured to walk down a street.   435
As for your humble servant, my first task
Was chiding, crimination, finding fault.
Sweet you may rest assured was such a state :
A pastor on one side cut to the heart,
Aggrieved to see such wretchedness and sin,   440
And on the other side a people sunk
In wickedness, in degradation deep.
But God be prais'd, amidst this chaos sad
Some jewels sparkled, much to my surprise.
I spoke out freely, visited and prayed   445
Beside poor wretches, horrible to view,
Mark'd and distorted with some dire disease.
And after this, though sharp were my rebukes,
And frequent too, among the strong and hale
Abuse was all unknown, and gratitude   450

Beam'd in the eye of the rough artisan.
But time admonishes that I must close.
Another charge I held near Liverpool,
And thence was summoned to the midland parts.
As years roll'd on I watch'd a chance to turn   455
Back to the scenes where oft in early youth
I roved delighted, free from care and toil.
And thus was led my residence to fix
Once more in Tardaton, and there was found
By your good vicar and brought here to-day.   460
In olden time the Levite, if he served
Full twenty years, discharged from active life
Was deem'd at liberty to rest from toil.
And I, who had myself served twice this time,
Had with my wife hoped to have lived retired.   465
Obedient to the call your vicar made
I came this day, and trust your minister,
Disabled now, may soon his place resume.
No small inducement, rest assured, was mine
To see old friends, old faces, and renew   470
Acquaintance dearly prized and long since form'd.
Scarce had I hoped to find so many friends
Alive and healthy. Thankful do I feel
That in the providence of God so kind

We all are spared once more to meet again.   475
Some faces once well known I miss, but see
Others alive, and bless that gracious God,
Who in His goodness has prolong'd our days,
And given us thus the wished-for privilege
To greet each other and our thoughts exchange.   480
      He ended, and with many a cordial shake
Of hands, abrupt the friendly circle left,
For distant was the station, and the train
Was due ere long. The railway and its plans
Had all been form'd since there he minister'd.   485
On rush'd he through the lanes with eager haste
To catch the train, but frequent were his halts.
Anxious to speed, his heart could not refuse
The welcome to return, and say one word
To well-known faces hailing at their doors,   490
Radiant with smiles and full of meaning clear
That much there was to tell, could he but check
His hurried march. All were alike assured
Another visit must be paid, and then
Time would be given more freely to reveal   495
Their joys and sorrows, accidents and cares.
      Now Lindsey was divided : it was once
In thought, in politics, religion too,

United : quiet once her children all
Nursed in the bosom of contentment lay,   500
Adoring God, and enemies to none.
Now alter'd was all this.   Fresh people came
From various parts and new ideas brought.
These counsell'd mighty changes, but the swains,
The old inhabitants of Lindsey homes,   505
Outnumber'd the new-comers, and their views,
Approved by some, by others spurn'd, obtain'd
Not much respect, but village discord bred.
The change inevitable was, and so
Its consequences were, howe'er condemn'd,   510
The current of events no human skill
Can fashion or forestall, though in their pride
The kings and conquerors of earth may plan
And in their hearts say such shall be the world.
The mightiest and the meanest bend beneath   515
The sway of Him who by His providence
Governs th' upheaving turmoil of the world,
And bids the nations know that He is God,
No place or being save Himself unchanged.
The father toying with his infant-child   520
Would wish the winsome creature to remain
A little girl in childish innocence,

From modish arts and affectation free.

The youthful husband, gazing with fond looks

Upon the beauties of his new-made bride,   525

Gladly would hope that these may long survive

And triumph o'er the ruthless hand of Time.

But age and wrinkles, haggard looks and gloom

Ere long creep in, eclipsing loveliness,

And care corrodes where beauty beam'd before.   530

Earth, sea and air, the stars and heavenly host

Pass through vicissitude, and know no state

Enduring still the same : this change required

As health for all, e'en as the restless waves

Drawn up by strong attraction keep the sea   535

Salubrious, free from pestilence and stench.

The very surface of the earth is changed.

Hills tower where valleys open'd to the view,

And corn-crops wave where once sea-monsters played.

Could our forefathers, who in Saxon times   540

Chased the wild deer across the open heath,

This world revisit, would they recognize

The England of to-day, as once their own ?

See'st thou all changing ? Ponder then, O Man,

The great, the final change that waits thee here.   545

Thou know'st not what thy after state may be,

Though bards and vain enthusiasts may declaim
And fill their heaven with furniture of earth ;
But here is real joy, if thou hast placed
Thy trust in God and His appointed means,   550
And safety sought beneath the Saviour's cross.
The child unborn knows nothing of this world
Unconscious struggling into life and joy,
And yet in God's good time finds here a home
Where guarded by his heavenly Father's care   555
Happy he may the path of duty tread.
Scenes of surpassing loveliness and life
Far higher, free from all alloy, beyond
The grasp of sense, await thy last great change,
The consummation of thy Christian toil,   560
Thy warfare ended, changed to change no more.
     Vain were all expectations that the priest
Who help'd their Vicar, should resume his charge
And minister again in Lindsey Church.
So Sunday after Sunday came and pass'd,   565
And still Nortonio found his lot was there.
With hesitation and distrust he saw
Lindsey again committed to his care,
Though light the duty, for his health had fail'd.
But still it seem'd to him who guidance sought,   570

The finger of a gracious Providence
Mark'd out that spot that there his charge should be.
So turn'd he to his labours once again
With all his might, and blessing from above
On his unworthy efforts sought forthwith.   575
Soon busied was he with his ancient friends,
Welcome to all and glad once more t' inhale
The breezes freshening o'er the Lindsey meads.
Nature herself seem'd to revive again
In all her youth, and warblers of the woods   580
Swell'd their lithe throats and cheer'd him on his way.
Few found he missing : those he sought in vain
Had pass'd from this world, save a very few
Who toil for trade in neighbouring towns had changed.
But a strong mixture of dissenting sort   585
Was leavening now the lump, and harmony,
Such as of old in Lindsey, reign'd no more.
Disquieted he was but not surprised
And tasked himself severely ; could this change
Have been, or been so great, had he remain'd   590
Firm at his post and never left the place
For benefice or fields of distant toil ?
Reflection cut the vain inquiry short.
The force of circumstances no one mind

Could stem or govern. Best he thought it then   595
To God's great glory to divert the tide,
And thus the elements discordant join.
No time was lost in disputation vain.
By all it was agreed the soul must be
The first of cares. All must combine and serve,   600
Howe'er their notions differ'd, the same God.
And now as formerly in all their cares,
Both great and small, he sympathised and found
Thus ready access to their inmost hearts.
Not long he labour'd ere events reveal'd   605
Seasons that call'd forth sage suggestion, hints
How to find comfort even in the grasp
Of hard-pinch'd poverty, and cheerful smiles
Well-timed renew around the cottage hearth.
Churchwarden Promnens soon his aid requir'd.   610
Some years with honour had his eldest son
Served in the yeomanry, and many a prize
For skill in arms or horsemanship had won ;
The young men envied but the maids admired.
And one before the rest his notice caught,   615
But young and inexperienced : still secure
His heart was fixed, a great event for him,
And much to be desired for all young men

Just entering on the busy stage of life.

The sage old warden, full of thought and care,   620

Deem'd it full soon for son of his to wed;

And could he so contrive, would wish his son

Should see more of the world and knowledge gain

Ere in the cares of family involved.

Little he said, but counsel sought alone   625

With his old friend Nortonio, who advised

No obstacles to raise, but uncontroll'd

Leave the glad lovers to arrange affairs.

Without delay the youthful couple came

And sought Nortonio's blessing, and his aid   630

To make them man and wife, all which was done.

A hasty visit to great London town

Follow'd, and soon with all propriety

They own'd a house well-furnished, which by death

An aunt vacated some few months before.   635

Right heartily to work the husband went,

And the young wife was busy in her home,

Whilst older heads regretted not the change.

Roomy and spacious was that house, too large

For folk new-married, without olive shoots ;   640

So deem'd Nortonio and th' occasion meet

To get a lodgment for himself and wife.

97

Soon were they quarter'd there, their house resign'd
To servants' care, while Lindsey and her swains
Engross'd their whole attention : so they wish'd, 645
Anxious to give them residential care.
With glad activity he soon renew'd
His old acquaintance, and the new-arrived
With special care attended, lest perchance
O'erlook'd or slighted they might deem themselves. 650
Some godly souls he found : one family
A valued acquisition was indeed
To all the parish.   Sorrow had been theirs,
Dark disappointment and affliction deep,
And Christian grace and holiness the fruit. 655
New was the place to them, but not unknown •
Their good name to Nortonio.   Once they dwelt
Not far from Clarebrook, near his ancient cure.
In simple resignation to the will
Of God, the father yielded to his lot 660
Without a murmur : him we Lemuel call.
With equal hope and faith e'en brighter still
His faithful partner kiss'd the rod that smote,
And acquiesc'd in all her Lord had will'd.
Cheer'd by their daughter Helen, and by one 665
Sweet sister of the father, Naomi,

Declining in the vale of years they lived,
Bent on one object, their departure hence,
In peace with all and reconciled to God.
Here was a gentle group, respected, loved,   670
Look'd up to by their neighbours, and esteem'd
By all the gentry round, as worthy were
Their virtues, manners, merits all retired,
Like some fair plants that cluster in the shade
And show their presence not by lofty heads   675
Or boughs bedizen'd with the flowers of May,
But catch th' attention of the passer-by,
Arresting notice by their sweet perfume.
Glad was Nortonio to find such old friends
And neighbours well deserving all his care,   680
He and his wife and this whole family
Enter'd at once upon a fierce crusade
'Gainst sin and vice of every kind and form.
But now a difficulty new and strange,
And one not easy to o'ercome, occurr'd.   685
Good Lemuel's wife wish'd every household there
Free from all discord, every father too
Loving and sober, to his children kind,
And glad to try e'en such amount of toil
As would secure to every soul he own'd   690

99

Comfort and health, from every want escape.
The wish benevolent, alas! was vain:
And well Nortonio knew that such a state
So near perfection ne'er could be attain'd.
And so he taught her that with all her zeal,   695
Discretion must be mix'd, allowance made
For early habits, rough uncultured ways,
Howe'er repulsive they might seem to be
To those whose lot in fairer scenes was cast.
Joyous the villagers their visits hail'd   700
And amply paid were all by gratitude,
Evinced in various ways, though far below
Their utmost wishes was the work achieved.
And now a labour to his heart most dear
Was well nigh near fulfilment, when reports   705
Of doings in his house at Tardaton
Reach'd vex'd Nortonio and his hopes destroyed:
So frail is human happiness, so brief
The satisfaction that we find on earth,
Though earn'd and sought for in the cause of truth. 710
Whilst he was busy in his rural charge
His house the scene of revelry became.
The sprightly grooms and lackeys, prompt to learn
And revel in the joys of Tardaton,

Soon found out damsels forward to be found,   715
By master and by mistress trusted much
But all unwisely, as events made known.
Sofa with broken leg and fractured chairs
Show'd conduct most unseemly, deeds uncouth,
Where meditation, prayer, and holy song   720
Had turn'd 'twas hoped, their minds to better things.
Roused by the rumours, in intense disgust
And hurried haste, the parson and his wife
Back to their home their sudden journey took,
Much to the wonder of the Lindsey swains,   725
Who knowing not the cause, conjectures wild
Form'd most unusual, and their leisure hours
For twice seven days were whiled away in doubt.

END OF CANTO IV.

CANTO V.

CANTO V.

Dark loom'd the future—In the womb of time
Events were labouring : and the deep designs
Of shrewd sagacious statesmen, now matured,
Were struggling into action—Tempests lower'd :
Men held their breath, and scared by rumours wild   5
Presaged some strange convulsion. He who once
The charioteer of Europe deem'd himself,
Felt the volcano rock his upstart throne.
Fires kindled by his own self-seeking crew,
Long slumbering, now burst forth, and hurried on   10
Commotions fierce, defying all restraint.
His uncle, once the blood-red star of Gaul,
The great arch-tyrant steep'd in human gore.
Chain'd to a solitary rock forlron,
Had paid the penalty of selfishness.   15
His vain admiring people too had groan'd
And drain'd the cup of vengeance, but not all,
That Nemesis required, had been discharged.
Wounds deep and many rankled in the soul
Of German chivalry—Forgotten not   20

Were all the insults heap'd in times gone by
On Prussia's beauteous queen and royal state.
Mutter'd the nations in dark dread : the noise
Of distant thunder boom'd along the deep,
And horror hover'd in the howling wind.   25
Safe stood the rocks of Albion, safe in mail
Of heavenly temper, from her Bible drawn :
And safe stood little Lindsey undismayed
Amidst the clamour of a world in arms.
Strange rumours reach'd her sons; ideas vague   30
Fill'd their untutor'd minds ; where Germany
And where was Prussia dimly they discern'd :
But France they thought was somewhere not far off.
Troubles more near at home and more their own
Held the first place in their domestic thoughts.   35
The leaven of dissent fermenting stirr'd
That small community so quiet once,
Placed in the heart of England, far withdrawn
From foreign discord and the ways of fame.

    Not long was Lemuel destined to enjoy   40
His new abode, though reconciled to change
Of place and scene, far different from the home
He once possess'd, his own for many years.
Deep secret sorrow more than sickness scathed

His tall thin figure, stripp'd of strength and health, 45
Marr'd but erect in his integrity ;
His faith unshaken : still most sorely tried ;
Assured that what his heavenly Father will'd
Must be the best, though all seem'd black around.
Week after week the suffering man declined, 50
The flesh all wasting, and the powers of life
Failing, each day beheld still more decreased.
Pale, weakly, with a humble face resign'd,
Once more he sought the church, and occupied
The pew, where he had loved to sit before 55
And hear of mercy through a Saviour's love.
Of public worship this was his last act.
Then to his house confined, his little room
Well furnish'd with religious books, supplied
Food for his piety and thoughts devout. 60
There oft was seen Nortonio, there he held
Sweet conversations with his Christian friend,
And calmly look'd eternity in view.
The wasting malady now wrought its way
Silent and rapid : efforts all were vain 65
To give the patient help.   His stomach soon
Rejected cordial draughts, nutritious food,
And all the aid that healing art could yield.

Ere long increasing weakness circumscribed
His movements so, that his sole dwelling place   70
Was one small bedroom, large enough for thought
To muse on mercies more than he could tell.
There with his family he loved to hear
Of holy things, though to the last degree
Of utter weakness and exhaustion brought :   75
Still never tired was he of prayer and praise.
Enlighten'd by the Holy Spirit, he
Could feel and gratefully acknowledge too,
Mercy and bliss unknown to carnal minds.
With gratitude he told his minister   80
How blest were they who godly parents claim'd :
The happy privilege that they possess'd
Who had been nurtured in the fear of God
And early taught their passions to control.
Though now no longer rich, yet happy still,   85
His sick bed tended by the three beloved,
His wife, his daughter, and his sister dear,
He traced in all his heavenly Father's care,
Pour'd out his thankfulness in words and looks
Of grateful feeling ; not a murmur heard   90
But love to God and charity to man.
His married daughters burden'd with the charge

Of infant children, living miles away
Did what they could to soothe his bed of pain ;
They saw the end at hand and fondly bade   95
A loving sad adieu, by faith assured
That all was right and they should meet again.
Nor long he waited : soon convulsions strong
Shatter'd the little fragments that remain'd
Of vital power.   Prostrated but resign'd   100
The dying man once more look'd round, and then—
Calm in the presence of the faithful three
Its mortal tenement the spirit left.

      Quick contrast follow'd in this changeful world
Of life and death, of infancy and age.   105
A choir of screaming babies rife and strong
With parents crowded in the little church,
Call'd on Nortonio to perform his part
And seal them all as soldiers of the Lord.
The joyful summons quickly was obeyed.   110
No obstacles arose when once impress'd
Duly with sense of duty sponsors came.
Sometimes a difficulty might arise
About the name or where the child was born.
One loving mother would her son call Tom :   115
" Thomas," the priest replied : " Oh, no," said she,

"Tom :" and no other name but Tom was right
In her maternal eyes ; so he was named.
Another would her son have Vanus call'd,
A name that sounded like the one assign'd   120
In ancient times to her, who, ocean-born,
Reign'd Queen of beauty o'er the Cyprian isle,
A name so heath'nish that the minister
Demurr'd to give it to a Christian child.
But after much discussion it was found   125
Silvanus was the name the parent meant,
A name both orthodox and scriptural.
From other parishes were children brought
Whose dwellings, placed beside bad pathways, stood
Nearer to Lindsey than their parish church.   130
Much loved Nortonio the parochial scheme,
And urged each parent in due course to seek
From his own minister baptismal rite :
But well he knew, 'twas dang'rous to delay.
And health and distance must be thought of more   135
Than strict adherence to a rigid rule.
Due consultation with his neighbour priests
Gain'd their approval : glad consent they gave,
For wide and straggling were their rural cures.
One child came from a parish more remote,   140

But of his coming ample notice gave
The anxious father, for his minister
Had shock'd his own and others' feelings too
By monkish oddities and Romish forms.
The child was brought with all propriety;   145
The parents well prepared, the sponsors too
To answer all inquiries and discharge
The grave and solemn duties then enjoin'd.
Prepared too was the pastor to receive
A furious missive from the angry priest   150
Whose fold the lamb belong'd to; but had gone
Where the fond parents deem'd the rite divine
With less of priestly craft might be received.
Th' expected note arrived : the answer was,
That if in humble mode, with decency,   155
Becoming reverence and an air devout,
Prepared to do what they then undertook,
The sponsors brought an infant to the priest
And at his hands claim'd Christian baptism.
It was, in prompt obedience to his Lord,   160
His duty gladly to receive the child, and do
All that his Christian parents could desire,
Thankful, rejoicing in their pious wish,
That long it had been, long might it be so,

The dearest aim of faithful ministers   165
To press into the fold of Jesus Christ
A willing people, and not drive them thence
By crooked notions of their own ill-timed.
This was enough : the Lindsey parson's views
Drew no more comments from the clerk chagrined. 170
    Then came the marrying swains, all blithe and gay,
Rosy and vigorous, bright with hope and bliss
Anticipated without base alloy.
Various the brides appear'd : some smiling came,
Some with a downcast and distrustful look,   175
As if a doubt were hovering in the mind
As to the future and the risk incurr'd.
Faith was not wanting, such as may be found
In youthful hearts rear'd in a pious home :
But where th' expressive eye, the thoughtful face   180
Show'd that reflection had perform'd its part,
Some trace of fear or shyness might be seen.
Banns were so often ask'd that prudent Snap,
The shrewd old parish clerk began to fear,
That no more spinsters would be left to marry.   185
For years together was no wedding seen ;
But latterly church-service had been charged
With banns so numerous that the people stared,

And public worship often was disturb'd.

The ancient bell that toll'd at other times   190

Was knock'd about most merrily, and rang

Uproarious, resonant, re-echoing

Through all the village, till the tell-tale smiles

Of all around the great event proclaim'd.

    All pass'd off happily, except the last   195

Intended marriage—that was sad indeed !

Poor Mabel in her inexperienced youth

Suspicious of no wrong, had shown her love

Too readily.   A fatal step she took

In yielding to her charmer, and the path   200

Of love made much too smooth, and now the toy

He once had sought, the faithless swain declined.

Great promises were made : fine ribs of beef

And rich provision for the nuptial feast,

All he most promptly undertook to find.   205

The banns ask'd out, the time was duly fix'd

For solemnising in the usual form

This last of a long list of marriages.

The maiden came herself and sought the priest :

He heard the summons : noted too the fact   210

That she, th' expected bride, alone assumed

The charge of all arrangements, whilst the man

Was seldom seen and only known to sleep
And sojourn there, a residence to claim.
He came a stranger from a distant part   215
In search of work and thus th' acquaintance form'd.
The wish'd for day was usher'd in with storms
Fierce and lugubrious: torrents of dense rain
Descended, ominous of cold and woe.
The mother and the grandam, widows both,   220
Clean'd up their cottage, furbish'd every tool,
Made all things smart as rustic pride aspired :
And there prepared sat with a few select
Of neighbours and of children, to receive
The ling'ring bridegroom and his gifts enjoy.   225
Much had the children heard of fruit and cake,
And now impatient grew, and clamorous cried
To taste the promised sweets, but none appear'd.
Amidst the pelting rain the priest arrived,
Cold, comfortless, and weak, and anxious then   230
To do his part without delay forthwith,
For long had he been suffering from ill health.
But ah ! no bridegroom could be found ! the nymph
Had made herself too cheap. The treacherous youth
Laugh'd at a distance : no fine presents came ;   235
No wedding feast or cake was there that day.

Sad look'd the visitors all dinnerless,

And loud were the complaints. Amidst the rest

Her grandam told the disappointed maid

That " now no doubt off to some other part   240

The youth would turn his steps, and there would wed

Some maid more fortunate : that she no more

Would see his face, and so might rest assured."

" Oh, no !" said she, " this cannot, cannot be,

" But he "—A flood of tears absorb'd the rest.   245

    Gay was the village with so many brides :

Mirth led the way and hoary care retired.

Light sprightly figures flitted through the lanes,

And gossip was all rife. The savings earn'd

Through many a hard work'd month were lavish'd

    now   250

Gladly and freely without stint or grudge.

The colours of the different garments worn

By bridal parties or their visitors

Enliven'd many a cottage, cheer'd their hearts

And banish'd sorrow to less favour'd homes.   255

Some few could have a house they call'd their own

By dint of mutual savings well employed.

But all were not so happy : some must wait

Till means were more abundant, and meanwhile

Abide with relatives or hire a room. 260
But these were matters of but small account
With youthful lovers, anxious to complete
One dear design, and settle down for life:
Happy in ignorance of the pain and care
That richer mortals have to undergo 265
Adjusting settlements and all the schemes
That lawyers can imagine, to secure
The property for ever; above all
To work out a long bill, that vies in length
E'en with the settlements that gave it birth. 270
But whilst this scene of merriment at large
Spread through the village and the neighbourhood,
Two Christian souls were sorrowing close at hand.
Schoolmistress Sartor who herself had taught
Most of the newly-married, now succumb'd. 275
Her malady had hung about her long.
At first a small lump on her side appear'd,
But little notice drew. Time pass'd away
And it seem'd ominous: no pain at first
But painful if press'd down. Still it was hoped 280
Time would a change effect and health return.
It was not so; through more than three long years
Slowly the malady increased, and then

What long had been suspected, now confirm'd
Beyond all doubt a cancer proved to be,　　　285
Her strength entirely failing, all the charge
Of school and children on her daughter fell.
The daughter, fatherless, herself had shown
Germs of consumption.　Weak, without complaint
Her mother she attended, and such aid,　　　290
As only could a loving daughter, gave.
Kind friends, a gracious watchful Providence,
Who for the sheep denuded of its fleece
Tempers the wind, provided and prepared
To bring prompt help just at the trying time.　295
Good Lemuel's widow ceased not oft to come
And comfort the schoolmistress and her child.
His daughter and her aunt were forward too
To aid in various ways.　Their timely help
Gave vigour to the school, declining now,　　300
In charge of its young mistress, quite o'erwhelm'd
With cares domestic and scholastic join'd.
Gifts from the vicar and the neighbours round
Flow'd in apace, most grateful; for the wants
Of such long sickness had well nigh reduced　305
To utter poverty this suffering saint.
And rapidly the fatal hour drew nigh:

Nortonio mourn'd, but saw that it must be,
And so he told his patient. She received
The gentle hint, as if she knew the words   310
He was about to utter; well prepared
To go whene'er her Heavenly Father call'd.
Soon came the summons : well her daughter met
The strain so trying to a loving child.
Close to the gate, that from the churchyard led   315
To her abode, were her remains interr'd.
And there Philagathus a tablet placed
Enduring, if in this world ought endure :
For it was made of iron, fix'd erect
So that each village child might mark the spot   320
Where lies the corpse of her who years long since
Had taught his mind and ruled his infant powers.
She knew but little : little had to teach,
But famed for discipline was she, and curb'd
Tumultuous passions in the youthful breast.   325
And now her child, a sorrowing orphan, seem'd
Thrown on this heartless world, forlorn and bare,
Helpless and houseless, destitute of health,
Yet happy in her troubles, calm, composed,
And unexcited in her hour of woe.   330
Her faith was in her heavenly Father's care.

' She had no fear of death : the world for her
Had few temptations : pleasures she had none,
But heard that such things led to sin and pain.
Unfit for teaching from the want of health,   335
She now must venture forth and face the world,
And strive, relying on God's help, to earn
An honest livelihood. So forth she went,
And some would deem hers was a cheerless life ;
But on her steps a watchful Providence   340
Waited, and smooth'd the way.   Round this poor soul
Whom proud and wealthy souls disdain'd to own
As Christian sister, angel-bands kept guard,
Peers of the universe her ministers.
Soon found Nortonio in a friendly home   345
Close to his own abode, an easy place,
Just suited for the girl, where one kind soul
And two fair daughters, like herself in heart,
Could comfort the poor creature, and require,
Although they paid her wages in due form,   350
Only such service as her broken strength
Could yield, and not bring on intense fatigue.
Most lovingly did these young ladies help
Their weakly servant : carried water-cans
To save her strength, and studied to avoid   355

Her need of climbing stairs, her breath to spare.
Their good deeds are recorded and are known,
And their reward shall follow in due course.
But all in vain was human help; the fruit
Was ripening fast.   Too good for earth was she.   360
She fear'd not death: to her 'twas gain *indeed!*

 And so the mother and the daughter died,
Two precious souls, dear in their simple faith.
Some few hours ere the mother breathed her last
Nortonio read some parts of Holy Writ,   365
And for the last time in this world she took
A part in that most blessed sacrament,
Memorial of her Lord's most precious death.
Weak as she was, raised on her lowly couch,
She gladly enter'd into all she heard,   370
Serene and certain that the promises
Made to good Christians would be all her own.
The daughter, when so weak that service thus
Must be abandon'd, ere she left her place
To visit country cousins, call'd to see   375
Nortonio, now her friend, her pastor once.
She promised to return and see him soon,
A promise visionary, for he saw
Death stamp'd upon her visage, and full soon

She join'd her mother in the realms of bliss.   380
The world cared nothing for them, but their deaths
Were precious in God's sight.   Nortonio thank'd
His heavenly Father : these his jewels were,
Dearer to him than gold or silver heaps
Or all the honours that the world could give.   385
　　Whilst visiting these poor, these pious souls
Oft did Nortonio to his mind recall
Scenes of past life, where vain and courtly dames
Burden'd with this world's wealth and bloated, full
Of vanity, of luxury and pride   390
Stalk'd through their halls majestic, wilfully
Ignoring what the child of want endured.
Some few were waken'd to their grievous sin
And saw the error of their ways in time.
This was the exception : others labour'd on,   395
Slaves to their own inordinate desires.
One wealthy mistress, far too grand to speak
To lowly maidens, once express'd surprise
That the poor girl, the object of her gifts,
Was reconciled to death, whilst she was not.   400
" Why should she not be glad," Nortonio cried,
" When death to her is change from earth to heaven ? "
　　Grim poverty ! thy patient followers then

Share not an unmix'd evil.   Some good fruit
May be at times pluck'd from the crab-tree stock   405
When grafted with the kindlier apple stem.
Thy struggling people cumber'd with less care
Thou leadest to the brink that overhangs
The bridgeless chasm of eternity ;
And less unwillingly they leave the shore   410
Where nought but troubles and dire difficulties
Their portion was, whilst fortune's minions quail,
Writhing in anguish, trembling on the edge,
And shrink with horror from the bourn unseen !

   Suspended now was week-day work in school. 415
The pious daughter of kind Lemuel
Had form'd her classes for the Sunday work :
And help came from the neighbouring parish too.
Young Voisin, who in scenes of busy life
Had taken part, and once to commerce turn'd   420
His thoughts in London, glad was to escape
From civic toils, and health and rural peace
Find in the hospitable home, where dwelt
His uncle Kûper on high Blacon Hill.
Most opportunely he as teacher came   425
With voluntary aid, look'd up the school,
Gave to the inmates clear judicious help,

And join'd the lady in attempts to train
Some of the children for a village choir.
And now a notice from the bishop came   430
That in a certain town, not distant far
From Lindsey, all of proper age be call'd
To be confirm'd, who had not yet assumed
The vows their sponsors made in their behalf.
This summons furnish'd an occasion fair   435
To rouse both young and old: the first to teach
In mind and spirit knowledge of God's word,
The last to aim at, whilst the young were taught.
Church catechising long had practised been
At Lindsey : there old people long had heard   440
Truths wholesome and much needed, whilst the priest
Seem'd all intent upon his youthful charge.
Good reason too it gave him to renew
His frequent calls on families, and see
The mode of life each candidate had led,   445
And form some notion with all care and love
How far profession with true facts agreed.
Kind help was always ready, if sought out
In loving spirit; efforts too were made
By parents or relations, who with zeal   450
Would do the work, if such as could be done,

That their young friends more time might have to spend
In preparation for the holy rite.
Sweet reminiscences of former days
Occurr'd, when to his priest the parent brought   455
His child as candidate, and with respect
Most deferential, gratefully recall'd
How years ago he was himself prepared
When first Nortonio visited that place.
And now he wish'd the self-same minister   460
His child to train as he himself was train'd.
In work like this Nortonio help received
From neighbour Voisin and the family
Of dear deceased Lemuel, never tired
Of working for their Saviour and their priest.   465
Their servant girl a candidate became :
Her name Eliza Faithful well express'd
Her character, and happy in her place
Her mistress she repaid by love and care.
Oft did Nortonio at the houses call   470
Where youthful swains were labouring, and obtain'd
Some welcome knowledge of their ways and thoughts.
But well he knew these visits must be timed
As not to interfere with duty's call ;
Or furnish an excuse to shirk or slight   475

The debt of labour to the master due.
Oft from another parish some young man,
Known to Nortonio well, would wish to join
The party of young candidates, and share
His Scripture lectures and advice required.   480
    One placid Sunday on his way he went,
By one youth companied well-known to him,
Who confirmation sought. He minister'd,
Heard all his classes and his candidates;
But long before all this had been achieved,   485
Good Lemuel's widow, hospitably bent,
Had found that with a friend that day he came,
And so an invitation pressing, kind,
Was forthwith forwarded that they should take
Refreshing beverage at her evening meal.   490
Now long Nortonio had been pledged to spend
Some Sunday half-hour with the eldest son
Of his respected warden, and behold
How proud both he and his young wife would be
Their minister to hail and entertain.   495
Postponements there had been, and many months
Elapsed before the day was fix'd : at last
Arranged it was that this should be the day,
When his young friends and their old minister

Discourse long-thought-of should at length enjoy.　500
When now the message from the widow came,
Grave reasons urged Nortonio to comply.
Time press'd: her servant Faithful well prepared
For confirmation now appear'd to be,
Except on one point, which Nortonio deem'd　　505
Would soon be remedied, if he could gain
Help from the mistress to assist the girl.
He scrupled not, but called upon his friend
Again the hoped-for pleasure to postpone,
Which, kind as usual, he agreed to do.　　510
Thus set at liberty Nortonio join'd
His widow'd hostess and his wish obtain'd.
And well it was so, for no more alive
Destined was he to see this child of God.
Pleased at that hospitable board he sat,　　515
His young companion seated at his side
And three dear lady friends, prepared to join
In Christian conversation, as became
That solemn day, though then but little thought
That it would be the last on earth for two,　　520
Poor Helen's mother and her aunt so dear!
Pleased with one subject were both young and old,
The bishop coming to confirm, and soon

The junior members of the church prepared,
Allegiance to their Saviour would profess.   525
Good things before him on the table spread
Were press'd for his acceptance by the kind,
The liberal hostess, who with right good-will
Welcomed his young companion to her house.
And there they sat rejoicing, and felt free   530
From care, anxiety, and worldly thoughts ;
All loving, ardent for the good of souls,
Fill'd with a sense of thankfulness profound
For what they had done, little as confess'd :
All glory giving to the Lord their God,   535
And only wishful they could more evince
Their love to Jesus and exalt His name.
Oh ! happy is it for the human race
The future is conceal'd : could but a glimpse
Of what impended, then to them been given,   540
How would a curtain of funereal hue
Have hung about them and o'ershadow'd all !
Swift flew the happy moments : time was gone :
Their guests must leave them, never more to meet,
Though nothing further from his thoughts could be 545
Than that Nortonio should no more behold
This widow and her sister, whom he loved

And deem'd the bright examples of his flock.
He and his young companion reach'd their homes,
And rose as usual for the morrow's claims,　　　550
But ere the sun had finish'd half his course
Tidings arrived, that early, ere the dawn
That day had streak'd the east, the shouts of fire
Startled the village.　From their beds aroused
The drowsy swains, bewilder'd, half-awake　　　555
And terrified, not knowing what to do,
Ran in wild tumult to the scene of woe.
Through the crash'd windows of that house, where once
In former times dwelt peaceful Possumus,
Volumes of smoke now rush'd enveloping　　　560
The few faint gleams of light that broke the gloom.
There by their cries they recognized full soon
The daughter and the servant girl, aghast
With horror, frantic, madden'd with despair,
Their garments all disorder'd, soil'd and torn,　　　565
And hanging loosely as not made for them.
Soon stable lamps and other aids were brought
To break the lurid mass, and vain attempts
Were made to force an entrance, but the smoke
Burst forth o'erwhelming and all efforts fail'd.　　　570
Amidst the turmoil and the stifling smoke

At the same window near the garden gate
Whence the young woman had descended safe,
By grappling with the pear tree branches spread
That grasp'd the wall beneath, just then appear'd   575
An aged woman, standing, half-undress'd
And looking calmly on the crowd below.
With countenance serene she look'd and cried,
"The Lord, good people, will provide, the Lord!"
And then from sight withdrew, whilst toil'd the
    crowd   580
Distracted, dubious, without rule or plan.
Thus precious time was lost: the master mind
To guide them to success was wanting here.
Ladders were sought but all in vain at first.
Whilst desperate with the thought that even then   585
Her mother might from suffocation die,
The daughter rashly tried to scale the wall
By clinging to the pear-tree, but fell back,
Caught by the swains uninjured as she fell.
At length amongst the crowd push'd forth a youth   590
Who lately from great London had arrived,
And married in the village.   He had seen
Scenes oft like this, and for a time had served
In one famed fire brigade.   As captain he

Was willing to co-operate and give   595
Some guidance to their zeal.   The willing swains
Most gladly heard his orders ; labour'd hard
With pails of water to supply his wants.
And now a ladder had arrived, and such
As to the chamber-window could be raised.   600
Cover'd with humid sacks, his face all veil'd
With well-soak'd wrapper, rapid up the steps
He sprang determined, agile as a goat,
And jump'd into the room through surging smoke,
And snatch'd the body of the poor old dame   605
Kneeling beside the bed, but motionless.
Breathless himself, the body was so light
That he could bear it to the window, whence
With care descending down the steps it pass'd,
The head reclining o'er his arm, and help   610
Prompt to relieve him ere he reach'd the ground.
Thence borne across the road to Sombre's home,
One sigh she gave, and no more signs of life
Remain'd.   Placed gently there, kind women stood
And sooth'd and comforted, alas ! in vain.   615
Speechless from grief the daughter and the maid
Wiped the dear face and scatter'd dress arranged.
Back to the burning house the bearers flew,

Aud now a cry arose, "Where was the aunt"?
Till then one thought had occupied all minds,   620
The rescue of the mother, that achieved,
Returning suddenly they call'd to mind
That high up in the back, behind the house,
The aunt had slept, and there she doubtless was.
On rush'd the fireman, follow'd by a train   625
Of zealous helpmates.   Scarce the ladder reach'd,
The back room window was so far aloft.
Now she was taller than the mother, placed
Not easy to approach, and now well-nigh
His strength had been exhausted.   Two bold boys, 630
Active and vigorous, volunteer'd their aid,
And in wet garments follow'd up the steps.
'Twas well they did so, for the fireman scarce
His footing could maintain.   The sturdy youths
Upheld him bravely, ready strength supplied,   635
Though smother'd by the smoke and parch'd with heat.
One desperate plunge they made, and then they found
The hapless woman kneeling at her bed,
Fix'd and inanimate, a lifeless form,
A shawl thrown o'er the shoulders, both her hands 640
Gloved, slippers on her feet, all decently
Composed, and bent as if at prayer she died.

Great was the effort now required to pass
The helpless body down the ladder steep:
But will there was not wanting, and success   645
Crown'd the attempt, though choked were all the three,
And ill and useless for some little time.
The corpse was carried tenderly and placed
Beside the mother: there they both reposed
For ever free from this world's toil and pain.   650
      Meanwhile the news had spread, and people came
From different parts to help and to inquire.
The youngest son of Promnens, in hot haste,
Call'd from his dreams abruptly, booted, spurr'd,
Urged his best courser at its utmost speed   655
To Guerrick for the engine, and it came,
Prompt and equipp'd, and ample work perform'd:
But the chief loss, the loss of two dear lives,
Ere it could come, was placed beyond all help.
At length the morning light reveal'd the scene ˙   660
Dismal and hopeless: black and charr'd it seem'd,
Disfigured, windows quite destroy'd, and doors
Hanging in fragments, whilst a horrid smell
At times forth-issuing fumed the place around.
Soon fell the fire beneath the drenching rain   665
Pour'd on it by the engine: here and there

Smoke burst at intervals, but peril all
Had disappear'd and vanquish'd was the pest.
Some bits of furniture were rescued now,
And in the barn disposed with jealous care,   670
Till came the son-in-law, who call'd had been,
But lived some few miles off. Delayed not he,
But came and sought his relatives in vain,
With one exception. Every effort made
Life to recall in mother or in aunt   675
Was futile. Overwhelm'd he stood and gazed,
View'd the dead bodies with a bursting heart
And big with anguish went to see the house.
And there it stood a ruin, blacken'd, soak'd
With water steaming o'er the heated bricks: 680
Dirty, bespatter'd, foul with soot and fire,
Like some poor wretch begrimed, that long had toil'd
In coal-pit darkness or the gaseous flue.
Hideous it look'd, a spectacle of woe,
Disown'd by love and hope, a scathed heap.   685
Where but a few hours since Nortonio sat
And talk'd delighted with those pious friends.
Was now an ugly void, where lawless flames
Had left the traces of their ruthless rage:
And this was all remain'd of what was once   690

The calm sweet dwelling of kind Possumus,
Girt round with shrubs and fruit-trees flourishing
In richest verdure, as if joyed the plants
To pay their owner for his watchful care.
Deep sigh'd the miserable man and gave   695
His willing labourers orders to remove
The wreck, and what remain'd to make secure.
Then turn'd his steps to where the bodies lay
In Sombre's crowded cottage : there he found
His sister and the maid with sorrow spent.   700
A vain essay he made to find the cause
Of this mysterious fire, but all the maid
Could tell him was, that "she was waken'd up
With stifling deep sensations, and she found
Her bed-room full of smoke. Her door unclosed   705
In rush'd a mass of smoke so dense and dark
That scarce with difficulty she could breathe.
Not knowing what to do she knock'd aloud,
And roused the mistress and her daughter too."
The daughter here took up the tale and said :   710
" Her door she open'd and a cloud of smoke
That instant enter'd and o'erwhelm'd them all.
In haste she closed it ; then her mother told
The house was all on fire : quick counsel they

Together took, and as escape behind 715
Could not be made, decided soon it was
That succour to obtain the girl and she
Must from the window drop, and then return
Her mother to release. Forthwith she put
Herself outside, felt for the strongest boughs, 720
For well she knew the tree that grasp'd the house,
And quick descended to the ground below
But little injured, for being very tall,
She reach'd out far to parts that best could bear
Her weight incumbent, but was bruised and torn 725
And sadly shaken by the final fall.
The servant Faithful follow'd with all speed,
But not so warily her way discern'd
And suddenly came tumbling in a lump,
Her ankle damaged and her side contused. 730
Then both besought her mother to descend
As she was light and little, and could cling
To the torn pear-tree with more hope of aid.
But firmly she refused and so they flew
And roused their nearest neighbours and return'd. 735
Time after time they call'd, but call'd in vain ;
Begg'd and implored her to escape at once,
And they would catch her if her hold she lost.

Once, only once, was she e'er seen again
Alive : when at the window she appear'd,   740
Utter'd a few quick words and then retired.
This was the sum of what the saved could tell.
Inquiry more he made but ne'er could learn
The real cause : it seem'd beyond all doubt
That in the kitchen parts the fire began,   745
But what the origin was never known.

     Sad but resign'd, arrangements then he made
That where they were the bodies should remain
Until an inquest had been held : but now
His sister and the maid with him must go,   750
And quit this harrowing scene.　In his abode
And with his wife, her sister, she might find
By God's great mercy even for this wound
Balm, consolation, comfort yet unknown,
Love mingled with her sorrow, love divine,   755
Hope for th' afflicted and the fatherless
Above the perils of this changeful world.

END OF CANTO V.

CANTO VI.

CANTO VI.

FLED now were many charms from Lindsey homes,
The charms of former days, when rude and blest
In happy ignorance, the labouring swain
Pass'd on his way contented, nor repined
For townlike luxuries, or fare beyond   5
His humble means.   Clean, calm in mind, robust,
His knowledge little, his desires as small,
If daily bread by easy toil he earn'd,
Enough he deem'd it for an honest man.
But now the spirit of unrest had seized   10
The younger branches of the Lindsey folk ;
And meek simplicity was only seen
Among the few old-fashion'd residents.
New-comers introduced their own new schemes :
Each had his favourite plan : dissent was rife.   15
Church rules were too contracted.   Boisterous zeal

O'erflowing from the bounds of Tardaton,
More fiery than discreet, found hearers here.
The lovers of dissent, brisk, fierce, and big
With vast designs to alter all mankind,   20
Now roused themselves to action, and found means
To hire a cottage and their meetings hold.
The newly-opened railway, though it touch'd
No part of the small parish, near at hand
Pass'd, and as usual brought both good and bad.   25
New notions, new ideas crept among
The youthful swains, till they began to doubt
The wisdom of their fathers, and to think
Themselves most worthy higher things to claim.
Three parishes extended to a point   30
Not far from Lindsey Church, and residents
From all the three came oft to worship there.
Some valued much the services, and held
Themselves indebted for the good enjoyed.
Others came forward with some new design,   35
And wish'd for surpliced choristers, and psalms
And anthems chanted in cathedral style.
But funds were wanting.   Welcome the excuse
To vex'd Nortonio, tired of novel plans,
Who with the vicar quietly resolved   40

That whilst with wise improvements life and strength
Might be infused, yet still the simple style
Characteristic of our Church Reform'd
Should be maintain'd, nor strangers interfere.
Most thankful did Nortonio feel to find   45
The vicar firm and Protestant, unmoved
Amidst the clamours for new forms and schemes.
Press'd with suggestions immature, uncall'd,
They look'd to duty, noted every change,
And prayed and hoped the issue might be bless'd.   50
Both advocates for progress, both well knew
That to old principles they still must cling,
And in the spirit of the age must march.
With endless talking for the good of souls
And doleful groanings for the sins of men   55
Much hoped Nortonio that some good would come
To his beloved flock, and kindle zeal
More ardent, more alive to duty's call.
Some, now advanced in years, and who well knew
Ere long their bodies in the grave must lie,   60
Seem'd little troubled that account must soon
Be given to God and judgment must begin
E'en at the house of God.   His boundless love,
The Saviour's merits and the help they hoped

From grace divine had occupied their thoughts;   65
But sorrow for the sins spread broad and thick
O'er many years of folly and of sin
He saw but seldom amongst such as these.
Painful it was and difficult to rouse
These veteran souls to vigilance, inclined   70
By age, by nature, and long habits too
To think but only of the passing hour.
   Close at the bottom of a pleasant lane,
Where join'd the main road, three young poplars stood;
And mark'd the spot, where in a lonely cot   75
Dwelt two old relics of the Lindsey folk.
Both now had pass'd the threescore years and ten :
The wife the older by three years or more,
Had well nigh touch'd her eighthieth year, but still
According to old usage Guerrick sought,   80
Walk'd all the way, and often undertook
The charge and labour of a tradesman's house.
Honest and cheerful, noted well was she
As nurse in illness, when some dire disease
Contagious scared the neighbours, and afar   85
In terror drove faint-hearted souls away,
Whose charity was only on their tongues.
Old George, her husband, left in charge to guard

Their household goods, their cottage, and their pig,

Felt solitude no burden, well employed   90

In in-door duties and his garden cares.

No anxious thoughts were his, for well he knew

His good old dame, to-morrow or next day,

Would safe return, and from the town bring back

Some creature comforts that were dear to both.   95

Both were industrious.   Years ago old George

Work'd for the village and the country round

As blacksmith.   Ignorant of books and pens

Accounts he kept not, but the farmers charged

Alike each year, however much was done.   100

Children they rear'd ; but these had long since left

And found employment in the neighbouring towns.

But oft they came their parents to look up,

And freely gave what little they could spare.

One fail'd not every Sunday morn to shave   105

His aged sire, and with his mother's help

Array the old man in his best attire.

The wife look'd on well pleased with sire and son.

Unfit for work long had he now withdrawn

From active life : his spouse more aged still   110

Blest with hale vigour, honest wages earn'd.

No savings could they boast : through many years

Both had been labouring and both had been paid.
What money wants at home did not require
Old George expended upon malt and hops.   115
Thus lived they, like the birds of air, devoid
Of care about the future, satisfied
With present wants supplied, and heedless how
The world was changing or themselves were changed.
Reminded by Nortonio that their lives   120
Their years foretold could not be much prolong'd
They acquiesced and often join'd in prayer.
Urged to prepare for his departure hence,
The old man meek replied, " He did do so
As well as he was able ; " shed a tear,   125
Fell back into a state of mind composed,
Easy, assured that all would yet be right.
A life so calm, unruffled, undisturb'd
By thought of this world or the world to come,
Contrasted strangely with the turbid wave   130
Of human passions seen at Tardalon.
Advantages it had, its evils too :
Good for the body's health, but in the mind
Prone to relax, dull sloth and stupor fed.
One Sunday morn Nortonio on his way   135
Had near'd the poplars.   Turning round he saw

The old man perch'd high in an apple-tree.
Surprised and fearful lest the branch should fail
Beneath the man, big, heavy with the weight
Of more than seventy years, he call'd aloud,   140
" George, could you not get apples yesterday ? "
" Oh no," said he, " I had not time," and look'd
As if escape he would, but there stuck fast.
'Twas plain the pastor unawares had come
And caught him in the act : stiff limbs and age   145
Barr'd the attempt, whate'er the wish might be.
A few years more and George one Sunday morn
To feed his pig essayed, and tried to speak,
But found he could not.   Fast the fit progress'd,
And down he fell.   Just at the moment came   150
Nortonio on his way to church, who rush'd
Up the steep hill and from the village sent
Prompt aid to help the wife, now left alone.
Recover'd for a time, George linger'd on
For many months, and without pain expired.   155
His widow, though bereaved of him who shared
Her joys and sorrows for nigh sixty years
Still wish'd to labour and retain her home.
And so she struggled on for some months more,
And took a lodger to provide the rent.   160

But time prevail'd.   Some faculties still good,
Her spirits cheerful and her mind serene,
Her aged limbs no longer could sustain
The task herself imposed.   And so she stayed
At home from dire necessity, and toil'd   165
About her garden and her well-clean'd house.
Early one day she told her lodger friend
She felt unwell.   A box of pills she kept,
Her favourite medicine : one of these she took
And fell upon her chair that instant dead.   170
          To these and such as these Nortonio hoped,
The zeal and fervour that he heard express'd
Among new-comers, would extend, and teach
How fire and vigour might be blended still
With primitive simplicity and faith.   175
But he was doom'd to disappointment sore.
The younger branches of old residents
Had listen'd not unwillingly to views
Broach'd by new-comers.   Grandsires look'd askance,
Shook their white heads, and doubted much the truth 180
Of what was said.   Sound sense and reason fell
Dwarf'd and dismayed before the blatant clique.
Sour Discontent, pale-visaged, blear-eyed fiend
Thrust in his hateful schemes, and caught the heart

Of young and idle, bent on something new.   185

Quick with the eye of love Nortonio saw

The change come o'er the village, saw and sigh'd.

Surprised he was not, for he moved about

The English world, and had beheld with grief

The love of novelty that now prevail'd.   190

Faintly he hoped that villages, withdrawn

Far from the busy world, would have escaped

The pestilential breath of demagogues.

Full soon he found that vain were all his hopes.

He look'd abroad, and saw e'en men renown'd   195

For honour, talent, equity, and sense,

Willing to lead a mob, and compass schemes

Opposed to order and the public weal.

Infected with the mania of the times

The new-arrived stirr'd up the Lindsey youth,   200

And wild ideas easily infused.

In many a cottage now were murmurs heard

And covetous desires to earn more pay,

Where but a short time since contentment sat

On every face, and round their frugal board   205

Parents and children gratefully enjoyed

Their food with thankfulness, nor wish'd for more.

Led by the specious tales some started off

To distant parts in search of wealth and work.
Enormous wages they had heard were earn'd   210
In those black regions where the chimneys tall
Belch'd forth huge volumes of begriming smoke,
Or clouds of vile effluvium, fatal blast
To verdant landscape or umbrageous green.
Amongst such scenes Nortonio oft had lived   215
And minister'd.   The nature of the work
To him was known, and so he gently tried
To show the people how unfit they were
To grapple with the labour there required.
The older listen'd, and the young some few ;   220
The others thought they would their fortunes try
And went their way ; but soon came back again
Dishearten'd, disappointed, and one died
Soon after his return, so closed th' attempt.
They found on trial that their fare at home   225
And scanty wages with fresh air combined
By far outweigh'd advantages they gain'd
In busy towns or noisome modes of trade.
But still undaunted the new comers urged
Their favourite schemes, and would not rest themselves 230
Nor wink at others in inglorious ease.
Peace and contentment they despised as sloth,

And onward rush'd as some high-mettled horse,
That with his rider strives for mastery
And champing throws his haughty head aloft.   235
Meantime strange things occurr'd. A blacksmith known
In parishes both near and distant round
For forging plough-shares with unequall'd skill,
Such that the farmers thought none were like his
Had found a spirit kindred to his own   240
Among the strangers, but of foreign race.
His plough-shares, highly valued, means supplied
For wild excesses. Broken through the bounds
Of decency, good, bad, alike defied,
That fierce virago join'd the man of iron   245
And reckless plunged into the dire abyss
Of drunkenness, of vice and sins unnamed.
Short their career : returning from the town,
Their brains all phrensied with the liquid fire,
Soon as, impetuous driven, they reach'd the turn   250
Where from the mainroad branch'd the village lane,
The woman madden'd in her fury lash'd
The wretched horse, that jumping o'er a heap,
Jerk'd forward the spring-cart, and headlong hurl'd
Its passengers and sundry bales of goods.   255
The man escaped with life and some rough cuts.

The woman, helpless in her drunken state,
Precipitated from the foremost seat,
Fell heavy on her head and spake no more.
The wretch, the vile companion of her crimes,   260
Recovering from the shock, upraised himself
And slowly sought the body of his mate,
Convulsed and quivering in the final strife.
Vain was his aid : for life was ebbing fast,
And ere the neighbours to his help could come   265
There lay the body motionless, and death
Had unmistakably his prey secured.
There stood the wretched man, a helpless sot,
Stammering and stuttering, stupid with debauch,
The man, who once in his paternal cot   270
Had happy been, ere he had known so much
Of strangers and the world's deceitful joys.
There stood he, while before him lay the corpse,
Exposed to scrutiny and stern remarks
From awe-struck villagers and neighbours round.   275
Too drunk to reason with, they sent him home
Placed in the charge of two strong aged swains.
The corpse they carried to a neighbouring inn
To wait the coroner, who soon arrived,
His part perform'd, and "Accidental Death"   280

Duly recorded.   To Nortonio fell
The next sad duty to inter the dead.
Then he to mind recall'd discussions past
With brethren of his church in times gone by;
How straiten'd they should be, if call'd to read   285
The burial service o'er the grave of one
Who died e'en in the act of flagrant sin.
How could they with a conscience clear, unhurt,
Thank God for having taken to Himself
The soul of one who had deceased in sin ?   290
Thankful he felt he was not call'd to judge
However infamous the case might be ;
And so could read the service, though he grieved.
Gladly he turn'd away from this sad scene
And sought for peace in visiting the sick   295
And helpless.   Lately to the place had come
A lady middle-aged, sedate, retired,
Accompani'd by a maid, but little known,
Though well-connected, as her relatives
In Tardaton were known and honour'd too.   300
To visit her Nortonio oft had wish'd,
But found access most difficult.   In vain
Time after time he tried, but some excuse
Was always made the visit to postpone.

Notes he had written, and polite replies   305
Had been received, and there the matter stayed.
He seized the occasion, when the village round
Was in a ferment from this sad affair,
To call once more and comfort minister.
Rumour described her as an invalid,   310
Who never ventured out, was rarely seen
By neighbours or the doctor: never spoke
Her wishes or her wants to visitors,
But through her maid communicated all.
About her cottage and her garden neat   315
Freely she moved, if she could move unseen.
The appearance of a man or even child
Was signal certain for a quick retreat.
From what he heard, Nortonio had inferr'd
Hers was a case of nervousness, that fed   320
Upon retirement and an idle life :
Happy perhaps if she had been compell'd
By sheer necessity to rouse herself,
And struggle for her bread : if real ills
Had held the place, where fancied evils ruled.   325
A cure seem'd hopeless in her present state.
A rambler she had been in search of peace:
From town to town she moved, and sought a spot

Secluded from the world, where not the sound
Of human voice, save of her well-train'd maid,   330
Could break the silence that she loved so well.
Fenced in with jealous care the servant caught
At intervals some grains of vagrant news.
And so Nortonio hoped the dread event,
That form'd the burden of the village talk,   335
Had now been heard of even in that house;
And that desire, nursed in a female heart,
To have the truth detail'd, would open now
The door that hitherto was always barr'd.
In haste he turn'd the intended call to make   340
And went prepared with sundry arts to try
To wean her from herself, and fix her thoughts
On higher things, but fruitless was the attempt.
She heard the cracking of the ploughboy's whip
In an adjoining field, and sudden cries   345
Call'd to her aid her servant, well prepared
For such a dire catastrophe, who thrust
A finger in each ear without delay,
And blocked each orifice against the sounds
That fell with horror on her tender nerves.   350
        Slowly but surely drop the curtain clouds
Around the eve of life, in sombre dress

The close infolding : one by one descends,
Friend after friend, till one alone is left,
The sole survivor of a numerous band.   355
So thought Nortonio, when he stood alone
Amidst the lonely graves near Lindsey church,
And mark'd the spot where lay the mortal part
Of good old Snap, his faithful friend and clerk :
And there, thought he, should lie his own remains,   360
When God had summon'd hence the immortal soul.
Musing he stood : the melancholy scene
Silent and sad accorded with his thoughts.
He look'd upon the recent grave of Snap :
There were his bones, but where was now his soul ? 365
Doubtless where dwelt the blessed and the saved.
Then, thought he, oft how had the kind old man,
Like an old butler, waited and supplied
His various needs, while they together held
A friendly chat about the parish plans.   370
Not long before his death, Snap stood as clerk
Close on the margin of old George's grave,
And watch'd the coffin as it sunk below ;
Whilst bending down he look'd himself mature,
Prepared to follow at no distant day :   375
Like fruit well ripen'd pendent from the bough,

And waiting only for a sudden gale
To separate it from the parent branch,
And add an atom to its mother earth.
Near stood the tomb by pious nephews raised   380
In neat and modest dignity, to show
Where lay the body of kind Possumus.
And sloping down beneath the yew-tree shade
Were many graves, where aged villagers
Slept their last sleep, no more to change exposed.   385
Thick interspersed were burials of the young
And middle-aged.   Nortonio needed not
Like Gray the Poet to conjecture here,
What talents they possessed, what mode of life
Best suited them, for well he knew them all.   390
Thankful he felt that souls so dear to him
Rejoiced in happier days, ere modern arts
The world had harrass'd, and brought in their train
A keener knowledge both of good and ill.
Blest in their humble lot they lived and died :   395
And fortunate in death their bones reposed
Beneath the cool green turf, and decomposed
Mix'd with untainted earth, pure, clean and fresh ;
Far different from the mouldering filthy soil
Turn'd up in churchyards hedged in by a town,   400

With human relics black, a sickening sight,
And smelling ominous of ages past.
And then, thought he, what wondrous providence
Was this, that he survived, so many dead,
Who once look'd stronger, healthier, younger too.   405
It was no act of what the world calls chance
But for some end designed.   There lay the bones
Of almost all the old :   few now survived
Who knew the village when he first went there.
And when he looked abroad for many miles,   410
His brethren in the ministry were changed
All round the village.   Two alone survived:
One to his bed confined, and one had seen
Full twenty more than three score years and ten.
Since first he knew the village, Hattham saw   415
Three vicars in succession :   three one church
At Guerrick, two another :   two Clarebrook:
And two the parish in which Lindsey lay :
And charge of Wolverdingtre three had claimed.
Alone he seem'd to stand ; for all, besides   420
Some two or three companions of past times,
Had disappear'd or join'd the world no more.
Was it a gloomy view ?   Oh, no !   'twas not.
The haven was in sight, high beat his heart,

Anticipating, when the shore was gain'd,   425
The end of sorrow and the dawn of joy.

　　Such were his thoughts, when sudden up the hill
Rose a strange murmur, and the mingled noise
Of many voices.   Looking down he spied
Three strangers in hot argument engaged.   430
Soon round the three a little crowd was seen :
New-comers and stray children form'd the mass.
Then ceased the three to argue : one stood forth
Their errand to declare and tale unfold.
Distorted action, gestures vehement,   435
Fierce declamation, full of empty sound,
Were meagre substitutes for common sense.
And yet they caught the minds of simple swains
Inured to credit all that reach'd their ears.
Grieved was Nortonio : at a glance he saw   440
He must pass by them on his homeward way,
And so be doom'd their ribaldry to face :
Pass them he must, and so he hasten'd on
And soon had hurried past the gaping crowd ;
But not so quickly that he did not hear   445
Fierce threats against the farmers, parsons, squires,
Which doubtless were thrown out his ears to catch.
He heard : he answer'd not : and went his way.

Tired with the hubbub and the prating crew,
Endless discussions about rights of men   450
And rights of women, and the steps required
To make all people equal in their means,
However tardy or however quick,
Nortonio turn'd in sorrow from the scene,
And with his friend Barbats, retired and old,   455
Sought conversation, medicine of the mind.
Some time he had abandon'd Blacon Hill
And fix'd his home a few miles from the spot,
For things were changed with him, and now no more
He joyed in Lindsey as in days of old.   460
He found him in his dwelling and began.

  "Barbats, old friend, the world is changed all round:
And you and I by God's good providence
Are spared to see a time when principles
And truths our fathers shed their blood to serve   465
Are toss'd and tumbled in one chaos wild.
Sometimes our clergy in such guise perform
Or celebrate the Supper of the Lord,
That doubt is left upon the minds of some,
If what has hitherto been error thought   470
In Romanists, be not the veriest truth.
Strange imitations of the furniture

And services in Romish churches found,
Are now so common in the English Church,
That e'en the staunchest of the Pope's best friends   475
Can with clear conscience in such worship join.
All discipline and order set aside,
They leave out prayers, the service mutilate,
Old forms reject, new music introduce,
And revolution e'en in things divine   480
They hurry forward with desire as fierce
As e'er bewitch'd the fieriest demagogue.
In two important points they differ much
From Romish ritual and its order known :
In no two churches is the form the same :   485
A Pope too they must have, but then each priest
Must be his own Pope, and not look to Rome.
Such is the state, I grieve, of our loved Church.
And looking to the laity I see
Confusion all, and nought but discontent :   490
Labour with capital in civil war
Involved : the rich suspicious looking down
On labouring millions, who to phrensy wrought
By hireling orators, conspire to earn
The highest wages with the shortest toil.   495
Thus selfishness appears to reign supreme,

And selfishness the narrowest of its kind.
But waiving these unpleasant themes, good friend,
Draw from the copious hoard, that you retain
Of rustic lore, some tale of former times,   500
Concerning Lindsey or the parts about.
Instruct, amuse, and friendly, thus disperse
The chagrin that possesses now my soul."

     Barbats delayed not, for he loved to talk
Of former times, and call to mind old scenes,   505
And so without a pause at once began.
" Changes there are, and changes there must be,
And we ourselves are changing while we talk :
Changed is the world on all sides : for the worse
Changed it has been of late : another swing,   510
And then we hope for better it will change.
The rent per acre was but three half-crowns,
When I a young man first began to farm.
For many years the rent has tripled been.
Fenced in is now the land, where all lay plain   515
And open to stray cattle. Corners now
Must be improved, and copse-wood all grubb'd up.
Close must the farmer reckon for his work
And seek economy in all his points.
How different must the country round have been   520

When lived those reverend and most worthy priests
Whom we were speaking of when last we met.
The vicar one of Snitterchamps well known,
The other Hattham's curate many years.
Both had a taste for learning, and bequeath'd   525
Some feeble essays for poetic fame.
But in their day much good they did and preach'd
Sound doctrine Scriptural and Protestant.
And would that parsons scatter'd through the width
Of England's parishes did now the same.   530
The priest at Snitterchamps tried hard to smooth
The roughness of his people; with success
In some few instances, but not in all.
A generous neighbour close at hand had kill'd
A well-fed pig, and mindful of his priest,   535
Had by the hands of his beloved son
Sent to him a prime spare-rib sleek and fat,
Who in few words his errand thus declared :
" My father, see, this spare-rib sends to you."
" Oh," said the worthy priest, " you should have said   540
' My father sends his compliments, and begs
Acceptance of this spare-rib at your hands.'
Now take it up and backward find your road,
And bring it to the front-door with those words."

The youth obeyed and bore the joint away.   545
The parson musing sat and listen'd long
To hear the stripling at his front-door knock,
But vainly waited : up he rose and look'd,
And saw the youngster slowly wend his way,
Bearing the pork along the road direct.   550
Then halloed he : "Ho, hither bring that meat."
"Not so," replied the youth, "if manners you
Still wish to teach me, I will teach you wit."
Off went the pert young fellow, smirking, gay,
And laughing at the parson's loss of pork.   555
But nothing daunted the good humour'd priest
Still labour'd on to teach them courtesy :
And left behind him, which has now survived
More than one hundred years, remembrance fresh
Of what he did and what he wished to do.   560
Since he was vicar, steady as the march
Of education and improvement been.
The glory of old times can ne'er be reach'd,
For who can rival Shakespeare, who can paint
Like him imagination or the truth ?   565
But many learned, many first-rate men
Have shed a lustre o'er the Guerrick realms.
One lady in my day whose parents rose

By honest industry in rural toil
To wealth and competence near Snitterchamps,   570
Became the mother of two famous sons.
One stood the first in mathematic fame
Amongst the Cambridge students, wrangler first
And second wrangler was his brother too.
When I was young at Hattham lived a priest,   575
Known for his Greek through all the world around.
A poet too was born in Guerrick town
Who died but lately and behind him left
A name admired, but much I fear, not loved.
Were I to take you to the Midland Mart   580
Oh what a constellation I could weave
Of men of science, men of world-wide fame!
One of their body, when he sojourn'd once
In Paris, and was shown a curious box,
Humbly permission ask'd, and guaranteed   585
The model not to injure, that he might
Lift up a certain plate, and there he showed
His own name and his partner's, that the toy
Our neighbours held as proof of Gallic skill,
Had been constructed in his own workshop.   590
Whilst in this world so many heads combine
New wonders to create, and day and night

Some fresh design devise, there must be change.
Old-fashioned people like ourselves might wish
The world more stationary : ancient forms   595
Strictly observed.   Like willows to the blast
Bend we had better, rather than like oaks
Be rooted up by storms we cannot shun.
Now, Reverend Sir, oblige me in your turn :
Your life and ministry have varied been   6co
Much have you known of town and country life,
And oft have labour'd changes to effect
Where ignorance and sin strong barriers raised
Against the Gospel you desired to preach.
Cheer up the present hour, and let us hear   605
Some details of your ministerial work
In Norfolk or in London years ago;
Such as at Lindsey in my brother's house
You often told, when by the weather stayed
Or waiting from some cause an odd half hour   610
Fill'd up with anecdote and sprightly talk."
      Full of good humour thus kind Barbats spake
And with a smile his visitor replied.
" Varied indeed, good friend, my lot has been,
And varied too my ministry : much change   615
My course attended from my earliest years.

Change loved I always when sufficient cause
Existed for a change, the object good.
My residence I changed so oft that friends
Nicknamed me Rolling Stone; but change that springs 620
From mere caprice, from ignorance or whim,
Or even worse, from dark corrupt desires
Stirr'd up by demagogues and hirelings vile,
Great zeal affecting for the public good,
Their own self-interest foremost to secure,   625
Such change as this bears fruit but little worth.
Change let us have from ignorance to light,
From sin to righteousness, and let us change
As fast as fierce reformer ever wished
The toil and object of my life has been   630
Such changes to effect, but bear in mind
Our master's prime injunction full and brief.
" Be wise as serpents, harmless e'en as doves."
Boldness in wisdom is a precious gift,
Boldness in folly ruin antedates.   635
In these our times accelerated is
The tide of changes with redoubled speed;
From two chief causes : one, the railway schemes,
The other, wealth diffused through every rank.
A patriot or a wise man cannot stay   640

These changes, but may guide them for the best :
This is what with God's blessing we should do.
As for myself, the field of toil with me
For forty years in various spheres has been.
In parishes with populations small   645
And populations numerous, rough, uncouth.
At different times my lot has been to watch
From thirty thousand to three hundred souls.
The larger number as in London vain
Was every effort to inspect and know :   650
The minister with all his zeal perform'd
Religious rites to masses most unknown.
If sometimes strange events, if even fraud
Were practised, priest and clerk alike were foil'd.
Especial care the marriages required.   655
And after all our care, manœuvres shrewd
To gull both clerk and parson were achieved,
And with success I doubt not much were crown'd.
In one place where as rector I took charge
The marriages so many were, that though   660
It was my luck to have a clerk, the prime
Of parish clerks, in conduct and in skill ;
Yet more than one full hour was oft required
The newly married names to register.

And often difficulties strange arose   665
About the spelling or the residence.
One woman I remember to a stand
Brought all on one occasion : she knew not
For certainty her real name, but thought
It Wilkinson, for short was Wilkins call'd ;   670
And Wilkins was the name in publish'd banns,
And so by it was duly registered.
Sometimes in visiting the sick a case
Occurr'd, that needed patience and much care.
A clever tradesman, young, yet fully primed   675
With skeptic arguments required my aid.
Ill, yet well able to dispute, he lay
Upon his bed, expecting every week
To be his last. Most gloomy were his views :
Little was he inclined to put much faith   680
In promised mercies; far too good for him
Was such redemption as God's word unfolds.
He deem'd it all but priestcraft well got up
To cheat the people with delusive hopes.
With great forbearance listening to his words,   685
Though then much press'd for time, I gain'd his ear.
I reason'd from the scriptures; but most loath
Was he to listen to some arguments.

The boundless nature of Almighty love,

And mercy welling from the heart of God,   690

Oft to my grief were press'd on him in vain.

His sins he spoke of as most grievous, dire,

And pardon hopeless.   In reply I urged

Isaiah's words—" Though scarlet be your sins,

Yet they shall be as white as snow, though red   695

Like crimson, they shall be as wool."   He said

" How know I that Isaiah was a true,

An honest prophet, for you know we read

Of prophets false, who wilfully deceived,

And by what pains can I the point attain,   700

That he in this announcement spake the truth."

" Prophets," I said, " must stand like other men,

Or fall in credit as results shall show,

And we must judge them by the fruits they bear."

Then long was conversation to point out   705

How some were godly prophets, and how some

Like Balaam, were corrupt, depraved and loved

The wages of unrighteousness.   At length

By God's great help, his prejudice o'ercome

He yielded to conviction and I left   710

Him still surviving, for in mercy he

Was spared to live, and, I trust, others teach.

Some time from Nonconformist's I received.
Judicious help, and thankful I record
The debt due to their love and earnestness.   715
Two brethren, who dissented from our church,
In Norfolk regular attendants were
At morning service on each sabbath day.
One man of energy our postman was:
His letters to deliver fourteen miles   720
He daily walk'd, and shoemaker by trade
Fill'd up his hours by labours at the last.
But not contented with vocations two,
Odd times he seized to pray and to expound
And stir up piety in country folk.   725
Oft was he seen with pencil in his hand
Most busy in the gallery, alive
To every sentence from the pulpit heard.
'Twas said, and I was told that he took down
Hints from my sermons and in houses near   730
Pour'd forth the same in a stentorian voice ;
Compelling by his vehemence and might
Attention from his hearers all around.
The other friend who was a hearer too,
A hatter was by trade, but often preach'd.   735
Both men were truly pious, both behaved

Like real Christians, and their master served
As far as means and talent would permit.
The parish needed all that men could help
And all the grace and mercy of our God ;   740
For it was sore beset with drunkenness,
And other vice from local causes sprung.
I and Dissenters lived so friendly there
That all were seen at Church, and ere I left,
Though numerous was the flock, the parish large   745
Not more than ten or twelve profess'd dissent :
And these were Hyperbaptists ; what their creed
And what it meant I never understood.
Now glad am I that to your house I came,
Good neighbour : somewhere Solomon well said,   750
"Iron sharpeneth iron ; and so the countenance
A man doth sharpen of his friend," and you
Have sharpen'd both my wit and countenance.
For whilst you reason'd and more fully show'd
What well I knew before, the need there was   755
Of changes in us all, it seem'd to me,
That I complain'd of what with reason too
Others might urge ; that my peculiar views
Must be abandoned for the general good.
And now this wisdom gain'd, this little store   760

Of selfishness stripp'd off, I go my way
More reconciled to changes, more disposed
With gratitude those blessings to enjoy
That still are ours by God's good providence.
One change awaits us all, one mighty change: 765
Be it our care for this to be prepared,
Strong in the faith of Christ, with armour proof
Against the world the devil and the flesh,
Assured that through our Head we shall be more
Than conquerors, and triumph at the last.   770
With such a prospect let us fear no change
That here awaits us—so, good friend, farewell.

END OF CANTO VI.

THE RESURRECTION.

I.

TIMES of triumph now are nigh ;
    Gain'd at length is victory !
Earth convulsed hath felt the throes
Of a birth she must disclose.
Joyful at his Lord's commands
By the tomb the angel stands :
The huge stone he rolls away,
Rolling like a child at play,
Easy as an infant boy
Rolls across the floor his toy.
Then thereon he takes his seat,
And beholds before his feet
Arm'd and armour, shield and spear,
Prostrate thrown in panic fear.
Vain their efforts to retire :
Face like lightning, eye like fire
Shot a terror through each heart,
Terror words cannot impart—
They as helpless as the dead,
Quaking lie, before him spread.
Human eye must not behold,
Human tongue must not unfold
What within that tomb is done,
Known but to the Holy One.*

* The reunion of the soul and body of our Saviour was a fact which probably neither the eye nor the mind of man in their present state could comprehend.

II.

Far th' infernal hosts are fled :
Jesus rises from the dead !
Satan dares no more be seen
Near that grand, that glorious scene.
Victor o'er His hellish foes
From the tomb the Saviour goes :
That torn body ris'n and free
Chosen witnesses must see.
To the women, struck with dread,
" He is ris'n," the angel said,
" He is not here ; fear not ye,
" Where the Lord lay, come and see :
" Quickly seek His friends and say
" That the Lord hath ris'n this day."
Hence they with great joy and fear
Run to tell each comrade dear ;
But before they tell their tale,
Jesus meets and cries, " All hail."
Welcome was the well-known voice,
Clinging to Him they rejoice :
Worship Him, and hold His feet,
And believe with joy complete.
" Would," He said, " my friends see me,
" Let them go to Galilee."

172

III.

On the road two brethren sped.
Musing on the loved One dead.
Two who trusted once that He
Israel from his foes would free ;
All their expectations now
' Fell before that crushing blow.
While they then their doubts express'd,
Jesus join'd them and address'd.
Holden were their eyes and they
Did not know Him all the way :
But when told the cause of woe
Graciously He deign'd to show,
That the Christ foretold of yore
Must bear all they did deplore,
Ere He enter'd heaven again
And resumed His glorious reign.
Rapt and charm'd they Him detain'd
And to stay with them constrain'd :
Bread He took and bless'd and brake
Calling on them to partake.
Something in His words and mode
Him their much-lov'd Master show'd.
Recognition flash'd delight
Whilst He vanish'd out of sight.

IV.

That same hour those two return'd ;
For to tell their friends they burn'd :
Them they quickly found, and heard
How to Simon He appear'd.
In reply the two display
How he argued by the way,
And in breaking of the bread
Made it known He was their Head.
Whilst the brethren wondering tell
Of events they knew so well,
Jesus in the midst was seen
Rendering more perplex'd the scene.
Mild He labours to remove
Doubts and fears and kindle love,
With a look benign He stands,
Showing both His feet and hands.
" Handle me," He said, " and see,
" Flesh and bones belong to me :
" Spirits have not such as these :
" Why be troubled ?   Be at ease—"
Then He deign'd to take some meat
And before them He did eat.
Through their minds fresh wonder ran
While He ate and talk'd as man.

174

Fully to their minds He brought,

How when with them He had taught

That all things must be fulfill'd,

Which concerning Him were will'd,

And by Psalms or Prophets old

Or Moses' ancient Law foretold.

Then their understanding He

Open'd and gave them to see

How to Him and none beside

Scripture words of God applied.

"Thus," said He, " those words declare

" Fully what the Christ must bear :

" He must die, and as He said,*

" Rise the third day from the dead.

" Then His people must make known

" Safety in His name alone,

" And to turn men from their sin

" At Jerusalem begin.

" All these things ye know full well.

" To the world these tidings tell.

" Lo ! I send the promise too

" Of my Father upon you :

" In the city now remain

" Till fresh power from heaven ye gain.

* Matthew, ch. xvi., v. 21 ; and Matthew, ch. xvii., v. 23

VI.

When to His disciples now
Jesus first Himself did show,
One call'd Thomas was away,
And saw not the Lord that day.
Those who saw, with one accord
Told him, " We have seen the Lord."
" In His hands except I see
" And feel marks of nails," said he
" And His side my hand receive
" Thrust in, I will not believe."
  Eight days after came the Lord,
  And held Thomas to his word.
" Hither reach thy hand," He cried,
" Thrust it too into My side ;
" Be not faithless but believe."
  Thomas did the truth perceive,
  Instant he his faith proclaim'd
  And, " My Lord and God," exclaim'd.
" Thou hast seen Me, therefore thou
" Hast believed," said Jesus now :
" Blessed are the faithful few
  Who believe, but not like you
" Have seen—their Lord." Thus in love
  He the doubtful did reprove.

Cease, ye sceptics, cease your strife—
Hail triumphant Lord of life!
With Thine own, Thy holy hand,
Thou hast foil'd th' infernal band,
And the pangs of death o'ercome
Ris'n victorious from the tomb!

Thine the triumph, Thine the might
Endless bliss to bring to light.
Thou dost to Thy ransomed fold
Heaven and deathless life unfold.

Foes all cast beneath Thy feet
Soon Thy conquests shall complete.

Thee eternal joys await,*
Thee all nations celebrate,†
Thee in every place and clime
Men shall bless throughout all time,
And when time shall be no more
Magnify Thee and adore.

Circling round Thy throne on high
With the angels they shall cry,
Cherubim and Seraphim
Swell the everlasting hymn:
Join Thy praises to proclaim
And exalt Thy glorious name.

* "Shall see of the travail of His soul and be satisfied."—Isaiah liii., v. 11.
† Psalm cii., vs. 15 to 22, &c.; and Romans xiv., v. 11.

VIII.

Faithless men must still be found,
Faithless though the truth abound.
Their loved Lord the brethren see
As was told in Galilee :
And their faith still to maintain
Jesus re-appears again.
Peter and his fishing crew
All in vain their toil pursue,
Till the Lord stood on the shore
And ensured success once more.*
Fishes many, great in size,
Fill'd the net, a wondrous prize !
Common was to all the thought,
This success the Lord had brought.
Peter plunged into the tide
Quickly sought his Master's side ;
Whilst the net his little band
In their vessel drew to land.
Soon then as they left the sea,
On the shore a fire they see,
Fish thereon and near some bread.
" Come and dine," then Jesus said.
None durst ask Him, Who art Thou ?
Knowing He was Jesus now.

---

* A second time securing a large draught of fishes.   Compare LUKE v.,
vs. 4 to 9, with JOHN xxi., vs. 3 to 7.

Love divine the banquet spread ;
There was fish and there was bread,
And a feast beyond compare,
For the risen Lord was there!
There was peace and righteousness
Glimpse of Eden happiness :
Looks of kindness and of grace
Beaming from that heavenly face,
Soft descending as the dew,
Comforted those chosen few.
Gladness, gratitude and love
In their hearts together strove :
Whilst to speak the brethren long
Awe restrain'd each eager tongue.
Holy silence reign'd around ;
Heaven-born joys the banquet crown'd.
Angels in that feast of grace
Might have coveted a place.
No contention them assail'd
Harmony with all prevail'd.
Each with ardour strove to please—
" Dost thou love Me more than these ? "
Jesus asked, he who denied,
Once his Master now replied.

"Yea, Lord, I love Thee full well;
"This Thou know'st and Thou canst tell
"How I love Thee." Then said He,
"Feed my lambs, thus honour Me."
  Silently in awe they heard
  Him they honour'd and revered;
  Nor presumed to speak their mind:
  He their secret thoughts divined.
  And again to Peter cried,
"Dost thou love Me?" He replied:
"Yea, Lord, I love Thee and trow
"That I love Thee, Thou dost know."
"Feed my sheep," then said the Lord:
  All in silence heard the word.
  Jesus ask'd again, "Dost thou,
"Son of Jonas, love Me now?"
  Grieved was Peter, when said He
  The third time, "Dost thou love Me?"
"Lord," said he, "Thou know'st all things,
"Of our thoughts the secret springs,
"What I feel I need not show
"That I love Thee, Thou dost know."
  This spake he with bursting heart
  Of his feelings to tell part.

Once again the Saviour said,
" Feed my sheep," and then He led
Peter's thoughts to future time,
When with zeal and faith sublime
He should gladly life resign
In his Master's cause divine.
" Verily when thou wast young
" Thou didst gird thyself, and strong
" Whither thou wouldst walk, didst go,
" But when age and time of woe
" Overtake thee, then thy hands
" Thou shalt stretch as far as bands
" May permit thee undeterr'd ;
" But another thee shall gird,
" And indeed shall carry thee
" Where thou wouldst not wish to be."
Thus the Lord in mercy spake,
And foretold that for His sake
He a painful death should die
And his God thus glorify.
From his Master as it fell
Every word he mark'd full well.
Jesus saw, then added He
One brief mandate, " Follow Me."

XII.

Glory to our God rehearse,
Glory through the universe!
All was once divinely good:
Man in holy beauty stood.
Heaven and earth in chorus rang,
While their Maker's praise they sang:
Love and joy and happiness
All their creatures did possess.
Envious soon the fiends of hell
Plotted, and their victim fell.
Now has Christ, the Lord supreme,
Triumph'd o'er th' infernal scheme,
And giv'n man in heaven a place,
Not by merit but by grace.
For this gift then from above
Of our heavenly Father's love,
And the Holy Spirit's aid,
By whose unction we are made
Children of the Lord most high,
Let us join in one great cry:
" Father, Son, and Holy Ghost,
" Blessed God, our Strength and Boast,
" Holy, Holy, Holy One,
" Peace is ours, our vict'ry won!

"Thanks we give, O God of Heaven,

"Thanks for every mercy given.

"We owe all that we possess

"To Thy love and faithfulness.

"With Thy help Thee we will serve,

"And from Thee will never swerve.

"Thine for ever may we be

"Thine through all eternity!"

TO MY DECEASED GOD-DAUGHTER.

TELL me, sweet spirit, shall we meet
　　When our great change becomes complete;
When shaking off the pond'rous load
Of earth, we reach that blest abode
Where setting suns no more shall shine
Nor waning moons in night decline?
Yes, stooping from yon azure cloud
Sweet spirit, speak, proclaim aloud
The glories of that wondrous clime
Which thou hast reach'd in youth's first prime.
Say, art thou occupied in praise?
Do harps celestial join thy lays?
With other music round the throne
Does thy young soul pour forth its own?
Or art thou, as on earth, above
Busied in messages of love,

Concurring in the grand design
Appointed by the will divine ?
Oh, dost thou often watch unseen
Thy parents in this earthly scene,
Permitted to behold, and shroud
Thy gaze behind some lovely cloud ?
Though happier far than tongue can tell,
A welcome guest where angels dwell,
Say, canst thou from that radiant height
Watch o'er those loved ones with delight,
And scan the cycle that between
Thy change and theirs must intervene ?
Amid the sinless host that shine
Enrobed in righteousness divine,
Does thy young soul delight to go
Oblivious of this world below ?
Or dost thou haunt that stream whose flood
Makes glad the city of thy God ;
Drinking of purer joys than we
Can comprehend or hear or see ?
Lost in the wonders of that plan
That vanquish'd death and rescued man,
What views ecstatic does thy mind
In heavenly contemplation find ?

Absorb'd in all the glorious theme,
Thy Lord could love, create, redeem,
Can aught of earth e'er have a place
In soul so occupied by grace?
Oh! if with thee thus raised sublime
We hold not converse for a time,
Submissive let us all fulfil
With patience our great Saviour's will;
And joyful let us call to mind
Those gracious words He left behind,
To all who hope to meet again,
Wash'd in his blood from every stain—
To His redeem'd—"Thou with me
This day in paradise shalt be!"

THOUGHTS ON THE SEA-SHORE.

I stood upon the shore, and gazed alone
    Upon the restless wave, and heard it moan—
It was an emblem of this turbid life—
This passage to eternity through strife :
And much I thought upon the ceasless cares
That chequer life, and compass it with snares.
Mem'ry and fancy both were busy then,
And told me of the heartlessness of men :
How rarely love prevails—how few have trod
The path directed by the Son of God.
Nature inanimate incessant groans
O'er man's sad ruin—e'en the very stones
On this lone sea shore show the stamp of pain
And bear the mark of Sin and Satan's reign.
But man goes forward, nor will deign to pause,
Nor think one moment of himself, the cause

Of all this misery—this fallen world,
In one vast universal ruin hurl'd.
Spirit! that erst upon the deep did'st brood
And curb the chaos of the primal flood,
Shine in thy might, Thy vital beams impart,
And drive the gloom from man's benighted heart!
O'er the sad ruin shed Thy heavenly love;
Pour fire celestial from Thy throne above;
Where hell once reign'd let heaven itself arise;
Save the lost soul, and bid him scale the skies!

TO

COLONEL ELD,

OF SEIGHFORD HALL, STAFFORDSHIRE,

His Schoolfellow and faithful Friend through more than Half a Century,

WHO, LIKE THE AUTHOR, IS A LOVER OF THE CANINE RACE,

THIS LITTLE POEM,

As a very humble mark of sincere esteem,

IS

AFFECTIONATELY INSCRIBED.

VIVISECTION.

IN that famed town where Scotchmen love to gaze,
  And talk of wonders wrought in ancient days,
Whilst newly fashion'd to their hearts' delight
The modern Athens rises to their sight;
A knot of Savants muster'd dark and shrewd;   5
Their looks forbade all strangers to intrude.
Some smiled with cunning, some with strange grimace
Still more disfigured a most ugly face:
Their thoughts seem'd bent upon some deep design,
And men might watch them but could nought divine. 10
Whilst stopping oft and whispering they turn'd down
Some quiet streets and shunn'd the bustling town.

Close at their heels a little spanielran
Wagging his tail and fondled by the clan.
The pretty creature all along the way 15
Repaid their kindness with his love and play.
Nature impress'd on every limb a grace,
Joy in his look, affection in his face.
Form'd to delight, no snappish cur was he,
Gentle and docile, from all vices free. 20
All seem'd to love him, and he loved them all,
Quick and responsive to each loving call.
But one he clung to as a friend well-tried,
And him incessant with his antics plied.
A curious smile, sinister, fitful, ran 25
Across the sallow visage of that man:
And he who loved phrenology might trace
The workings of the mind beneath that face:
For passion there had left its wrinkles deep;
Fictitious looks the secret could not keep. 30
Pride, selfishness, ill-temper, envy reigned:
The knitting brow proclaim'd each smile was feign'd.
No wonder that his home was dull to him
Who found in pain a satisfaction grim,
Pain seen in others, for h'mself a sight 35
Which he could muse on with a strange delight.

His wife to please him long in vain had tried ;
Pale, thin, and sick, she lived on hope and sighed.
His children loved him not ; with secret dread
Heard his arrival and his presence fled.   40
But now he left all cares of home behind ;
Far other thoughts engaged his sapient mind.
A deed congenial now he had in hand :
Ripe for fulfilment was the scheme he plann'd.
Through months it was discuss'd ; some scruples hard   45
Had often baffled and his purpose marr'd.
But other kindred spirits he had found :
Success at length his perseverance crown'd.
And so with comrades pleased the feat to see
He hurried through the streets with secret glee.   50
     Ere long this doctor and his learned band,
Before a house, hid in a corner, stand ;
Then all suspicious look around, and seem
Like burglars bent on some nocturnal scheme,
Eye every passer-by and look askance   55
And e'en on children cast a prying glance.
Soon as the door was open'd in rush all :
Fond Tasso follows at his master's call.
Alas, the loving creature little thought
With what intention he was thither brought.   60

Confiding in his master's care he goes
And loves as friends whom soon he finds his foes.
And now around they press, where oft before
The joys of luxury they revell'd o'er ;
And whilst they pander'd to the appetite   65
In talk that smack'd of science took delight.
No savoury dishes now adorn the scene,
But sable cases on the board are seen,
And near them lie some instruments, that seem
Keen-edged, prepared for some mysterious scheme.   70
Not long they linger ; soon the dog they seize,
His master foremost, whom he loved to please.
The unsuspecting creature turn'd his eyes
And fix'd them on his master with surprise,
Mutely appealing to that harden'd heart   75
Why in such usage he should bear a part.
Unwilling still his master to resist,
He sought the well-known hands and lick'd and kiss'd.
Vain was remonstrance dumb or eloquent
To such a wretch on horrid thoughts intent.   80
And so the hapless victim writhed and whined,
While every limb the tightening straps confined.
Upon the table helpless, bound, he lies :
Views his tormentors with imploring eyes ;

Looks for a friend, but looks, alas ! in vain,   85
Whilst useless struggles still increase his pain.
But cruelty in various ways applied
Like sin and death is never satisfied :
And so before experiments begin
A cord is drawn around the tongue, within   90
The creature's mouth, close to the root, whilst hard
He struggles still their object to retard.
Then underneath the table round its end
The string is fasten'd, tight enough to rend
Their victim's tongue, if whilst the search they trace 95
He dares to struggle or to move his face.
And now with fiendish lust they gather round :
Consult and argue how and where to wound.
Soon it was settled by the sapient band
To make incisions near the ribs, right-hand ;   100
And so an entrance deep, clean-cut, and wide,
His master open'd in the poor dog's side.
The blood and groans that issued at the time
Unheeded were by such a mind sublime :
Reward to him was scientific fame   105
For all this torture and this horrid game.
Now curiously they note the important fact
How on the other side the lung will act ;

And when to gratify their strange desire
They see enough, that he can still respire,   110
They turn him over and the other side
With equal skill and cruelty divide.
Both sides laid open, and the vital force
By cruel art arrested in its course,
Pleased with their work they look, and watch how soon 115
Beneath their clever hands the dog will swoon.
Sobbing and tortured now in every limb
They see him suffer and his senses swim :
No pangs of sympathy disturb meanwhile ;
'Tis his to suffer, theirs to talk and smile.   120
Oft as he tries to move the smallest space
The cutting cord pulls down his tongue and face ;
And all the means by which he seeks relief
Add to his anguish and heart-rending grief.
But God be praised : more merciful than man   125
He put a limit to their savage plan !
Fast fail the powers of life and consciousness,
And with them cease the outcries of distress.
Insensible to all the dog falls o'er
And feels the torments they inflict no more.   130
    But anxious ere the vital spark had fled,
They hurry forward and release his head ;

Close up the open parts; unloose the thongs,

And gently raise him to assist the lungs :

Then watch him carefully to see how soon   135

The dog would rally from this death-like swoon.

Young was the creature; so returning life

Contended bravely in this deadly strife.

The opening nostrils and the quivering tongue

Show'd inhalation entering in the lung.   140

With rising sobs and desperate gasps for breath

He struggles, and escapes the threaten'd death.

Slowly his eyes their visual strength enhance

And on his master cast a wondering glace :

Whilst two young men, each with a watch in hand,   145

Observant of each movement, near him stand.

The point inquired for is, what time between

Revival and the swoon must intervene :

So notice of each second was retain'd

Till breath and animation were regain'd.   150

Sage observations on all nature's laws

Fill'd up the interval and left no pause.

The mutilated creature, half-alive

Feebly begins his sorrows to revive

And moaning piteously with gasping sighs,   155

Speaks to his murderers through his plaintive eyes.

His groans they heed not, but with pride accurst
Harden'd for fresh experiments they thirst :
So turn him over without more delay
And lay his belly open to the day :   160
Then make incisions and draw back the skin
To watch the action of the parts within.
Wide open are the wounds that they may spy
How in a living brute the inwards lie.
With microscopes and various aids of art   165
They pry into the secrets of each part,
Luxuriate in the search, as if at least
Mere mutilation were to them a feast.
Much scientific jargon, many a word
Which Savants only understand, was heard.   170
But whilst they argue, whilst they thus discuss,
The God of nature closed their learned fuss.
The miserable dog, whose fate had been
The leading feature of this sickening scene,
As far as sensibility and pain   175
Were there concern'd, died once and o'er again,
But now the spirit from the carcass fled
And stretch'd before them lay the dog quite dead.

  Ye hideous wretches, devils in men's shape,
Just retribution hope not to escape !   180

Think ye th' All-seeing eye shall see in vain
His helpless creatures suffer useless pain?
Was it for this that sovereign power was given
O'er brute creation by the God of heaven?
Ye maudlin students of false science, say,   185
What knowledge gain'd ye by your bloody play!
*One of your number well might long repine
And in his sufferings trace the hand Divine.
Whilst hope was high and whilst the wreaths of fame,
Busy he gather'd round his rising name,   190
The grave wide opening suddenly he saw
And death relentless claim'd him for his maw!
But pangs unutterable without cure,
Horrors incessant he must first endure.
The dire disease soon fasten'd on the tongue,   195
That very member he had probed so long
In helpless brutes; and then he call'd to mind
How he had lectured and had oft refined!
Philosophizing, while the creature's life
Was wasting fast beneath the cruel knife.   200
Alas! such penitence, remorse so vain
Made poor atonement for the wrongs and pain
Inflicted on the wretched brutes that died
The victims of such scientific pride.

* SEE NOTE AT THE END.

* I regret to say that the above account, as given in the body of the Poem and as respects an eminent Physician, is founded in fact. The experiments made on the miserable dog were such as are there recorded. The dreadful disease, cancer at the root of the tongue, carried off Dr. R ₊ ₊ ₊ in the prime of life. He bitterly reproached himself with having made numerous experiments upon that very member in animals still alive, and confessed that he had been led to do so from a desire for scientific fame.

GLOSSARY.

CANTO I.

10.—Possumus (Latin), intimating power, ability, canning: hence cyninge or cyng (old English) and king modern English).

12.—Promnens, for *prominens* (Latin), projecting out, gibbous, &c.

16.—Anakson, son of Anak, whose race in the Old Testament was famous for being tall, strong, and brave.

18.—Eric (Latin, *erica*,) heath.

25.—Calvus (Latin), bold. Calva, feminine of Calvus.

31.—Amnes (Latin), brooks, rivers, &c.

35.—Homo (Latin), man—a general term.

33.—Sartor (Latin), tailor—hence the common English name Taylor.

153 and 154.—Clardonis and Nortonio, derived from the places with which they were connected.

255.—Barbats (Latin), from *barbatus*, bearded.

CANTO II.

170.—Clarebrook. This is used as the name of a certain village in Warwickshire, of which the name, according to one of our most accurate and celebrated antiquarians, is derived from two words signifying clear and brook.

192.—Woven. The name of Webb is comparatively common in the Midland counties.

222.—Tardaton. Pope calls a certain river Vaga—no doubt from its devious course. So a certain river in Warwickshire, well known for its slow current, may be called Tarda, and the town on its banks, which is named after that river, may here be called Tardaton.

323.—WULFTAN. In one copy of the Saxon Chronicle the name is spelt Wulftan, but it is often spelt by modern writers, as in Stanley's *Westminster Abbey*, Wulfstan (with s). Another Saxon Prelate, who was prior to the Bishop of Worcester, was called Wulfstan.

CANTO III.

LINE

71.—GUERRICK. French, *guerre*—war, and English, *wick*, a terminal meaning, a habitation, as Berwick, Alnwick, &c.

150.—CURLIEU. Name derived from the owner, who lived soon after the Norman Conquest. The same may be said of Lindsey.

178.—HATTHAM. The terminals *ham*, *ton*, *tre*, appear all in ancient times to have meant a dwelling or something conspicuous, as a hill—as Laleham, little town; Leamington, town on the Leam; Coventry, or more anciently Coventre, town of convents.

CANTO IV.

LINE

262.—PHILAGATHUS (Greek), Lover of good.

661.—LEMUEL (Hebrew), One belonging to God. Prov., ch. xxxi., v. 1.

666.—NAOMI (Hebrew), One of a comely presence.

CANTO V.

LINE

197.—MABEL (French), My beauty.

411.—VOISN (French), Neighbour.

416.—KÛPER (Icelandic), from *ku*, a cow.

ERRATA FOR LINDSEY.

PAGE 29, LINE 60, *for* hugh   *read* huge.

,, 52, LINES 140 and 141 should be

Fierce from her chair she sprang : grasped with both hands
The besom stale that lay beside the door,

The words *both hands* belong to line 140.

PAGE 78, *for* LINE 177 *read* : What he and she had done
had given a right.

,, 87, LINE 396, *for* Hougomout *read* Hougomont.

,, 103, ,, 14, ,, forlron ,, forlorn

,, 109, ,, 161, leave out the word *gladly* in this line.

,. 112, ,, 232, *for* be   *read* he

,, 113, ,, 238, ,, rest ,, rout.

,, 167. There should be no stop at the end of line 713.